GRAN'S BROTHER'S GHOST

CHAPTER ONE

Then Mrs. James asked us to write about what we did on our summer holidays.

'You can't ask that Miss its like something out of Dickens,' says Sophe.

'I didn't know you were familiar with Dickens, Sophie, perhaps you can tell us something he wrote.'

'I didn't know he was a writer, it was just …. ' Sophe is struggling.

'An expression,' suggests Mrs. James.

'More like… something my Nan says.' Mrs. James likes stuff our grandparents say.

Ed, that's my brother, says Mrs. James is too old to be a teacher and we've moved on since timelines. He calls her James the giant Pterodactyl. Don't ask. I did.

'Because she's too heavy to fly.' Ed says things like that.

Nathaniel Collier says, 'Dickens wrote Oliver Twist and things they put on telly at Christmas,' which Sophe says is seriously sad and Nat should get out more. But she doesn't say it till we we're in the playground. I'm glad I didn't put my hand up. Mostly I'm glad because I was going to say he wrote Treasure Island but I just remembered that was someone else though I haven't remembered who.

'What are you going to write about?' I ask.

'The Taj Mahal,'

'You've never been to the Taj Mahal you always go to Spain.'

'You don't have to go there to write about it, that's what writing's for, making things up,' she says making it sound alright.

Then she says Luce, that's her sister, had a picture of Princess Diana outside the Taj Mahal on her wall for ages because she was iconic. Diana that is, not Luce. She says the Taj Mahal was built for someone's dead wife, a sort of giant gravestone. I'm impressed. I didn't know Sophe knew so much about it. Ed says I'm easily impressed. Ed is short for Edmund but everyone thinks his name is Edward. He says Mum and Dad might as well have called him Edward as it would have saved time explaining and by the time he dies he might have wasted a whole year just telling people that his name's Edmund not Edward. People think Ed talks like that because he's got leukaemia and he's worrying about dying young but he talked like that before he had it. My name is Matilda but I'm called Mattie. Sophe said, 'Tilly's better.' She tried calling me Tilly once, but gave up because the others just said, 'Who's Tilly?'

I'm glad Mrs. James asked us to write about our summer holidays because it means I can say about the ghost. The thing is I haven't even told Sophe about the ghost . I have tried but ghost conversations never come up. I saw him, the ghost that is, at my Gran and Grandad's when I went to stay with them because Ed was having a bone marrow transplant. Mum was going to have to spend a lot of time at the hospital as he'd be in isolation.

I said I didn't want to go and Mum said I didn't have to, but Gran and Grandad wanted to help. I can't see it's being helpful if I don't want to go and if I don't want to go why am I going?

But I do because I know its worse for Ed. Going to stay with Gran and Grandad or having a bone marrow transplant? No contest. Everyone's pleased about having a match for his bone marrow. I was just hoping he'd grow out of it. Isolation sounds more like a punishment than a cure. I try to think of a desert island which I think Ed would like but when I say that he says, 'Depends if you can get a signal.'

Dad says, 'You're never alone with in a virtual world,' I don't think either of them have even read Robinson Crusoe.

I am now going to start my story.

'When the 21st century was only five years old, I, Matilda Emily George, travelled from Yorkshire to Somerset to visit my grandparents while my brother was being treated for a serious illness.'

'That really does sound like something out of Dickens,' says Sophe looking over my shoulder. I looked over hers, it said. 'I was wearing an orange top and my new jeans with white trainers as Lucy my sister took my photograph outside the Taj Mahal glittering like an advert under the Indian sun.'

'Advert for what?'

Sophe didn't answer. I thought she night think I was being sarcastic but I wasn't. I just wanted to know. Then I saw she'd changed it to 'glittering like an advert for diamonds.' I couldn't think of an advert for diamonds but I expect there is one.

By now Mrs James had put suggestions on the board to start us off. When I arrived at the airport/hotel/beach.

'Where else might you arrive?'

'The bus station,' says Jess.

'Penguin thinks the bus station will save the planet,' says Nat. He calls Jess Penguin but not in a nice way.

'Trying to make Mrs. James feel guilty for presuming everyone's got a car or goes abroad more like,' says Sophe.

'That's good Jess,' says Mrs. James as though she'd overheard us and writes, Bus Station, in big letters.

I start again.

When we get to Ridgeway Road the home of my Gran and Grandad I think it looks a bit dark and sort of spooky, though I've been here before and not noticed.

'That hedge needs cutting, d'you think they're getting past it,' says Dad.

I was glad to get there, though not to be staying there. It's a long drive to Somerset though not very far actually. I mean it's closer than Spain but it feels further if you're not on a plane.

'It probably felt further still in the old days when you had to ride a horse,' says Ed. At this moment someone does come by on a horse so it feels as if we are in the old days. This isn't a ghost, just a girl on a horse.

The ghost doesn't come till I go up to my room, which is after Mum and Dad and Ed have left. I'm feeling totally left behind like I'm the one in isolation. Then I think what if Ed dies and I never see him again. I've never dared think that before. Like getting murdered, which I don't think about either but Sophe does. Once me and Sophe met a man who was muttering and looking at the ground, acting suspiciously anyway. He asked us what time it was.

'Don't answer,' said Sophe

'Why not?'

'What if he's a paedophile?'

'What if he's not?'

'It won't matter, he just won't know what time it is, but we won't have been raped or trafficked on the internet as sex slaves.' I hadn't thought that far ahead.

I told Ed about it.

'That was Clocker Wallace, he's autistic.'

'Does that stop him being a murderer?'

'Probably, he's only interested in one thing.'

'Like?'

'What time it is.'

Mrs. James says if you could try to concentrate on one thing at a time class we might get some work done. But I expect she'd be sorry if the one thing wasn't the one she'd chosen. I suppose Clocker Wallace always knows what time it is. I never know what to do next. It's like choosing yoghurt.

Gran comes upstairs with me to show me, my bedroom, which I'm sure was empty till she goes downstairs and then there's this boy. I don't think he's a ghost at first. I just think I'm in the wrong room. I think Dad was right and Gran's losing it and I'm going to be stuck here with crazy grandparents and a long lost cousin they've forgotten about.

The boy is playing with toy cars. He looks old fashioned, but not old fashioned enough to be a ghost or even someone out of Dickens. He's got short hair, but so do a lot of boys. His doesn't look like he ever tried to copy David Beckham. He's wearing a grey shirt and short trousers which doesn't sound abnormal but there's something wrong, its the material, the material's too thick. He's got long woollen socks with a pattern at the top instead of a logo that look like the only thing they'd go with is a kilt. I know one thing, I wouldn't want anyone in my class to see me if I was with him.

He's white, white like a European not white like a ghost but I think he might be a refugee and hiding in the house like Anne Frank. He might be an illegal immigrant who doesn't want to be sent back to somewhere with a war on. But I remember seeing refugees on television and they all looked modern. I remember because Sophe said her Nan had given some clothes to an appeal but she didn't think anyone would want to wear her Nan's clothes, particularly the ones her Nan didn't want to wear.

A ginger cat is sat watching the toy cars go down a ramp made out of a tray and books. The books are hardbacks, I couldn't see the titles but I know it isn't Harry Potter. I just know. Ed would say you can't just know, you know because of a reason and that we only make judgements on evidence. Ed should be a detective. I think of speaking to the boy in French as I do French. But I can't think of any, like being on a quiz show on telly. Not that I've ever been on a quiz show but when people don't know the answers they always say, 'Its different when you're on television.' Ed laughs as though its a bad excuse. But I know what they mean, like Karaoke when it seems like you know all the words because they're on the screen. I can only think of French when I'm at school, not talking to an alien in an old bedroom.

I was just going to go back downstairs to tell Gran, even if he was a refugee and then I remembered her saying, 'China into England won't go,' like it was a sum, when they said about some Chinese refugees on the News. She might not want him even though he's not Chinese. Well not in her house.

I'm a bit worried about getting undressed even though the boy isn't looking at me. It's as though he doesn't know I'm there. Perhaps he's autistic, perhaps he's only interested in one thing? The toy cars I mean, not what time it is.

'Are you alright up there?' its Gran calling out.

I look round and the boy has disappeared and that's when I think he's a ghost. I suppose I should be scared but I'm not. It's more like I've come here especially to see him. As though it was advertised, 'Come to our Haunted House and Prepare to be Amazed.' Which means you won't be amazed as you're expecting to see a ghost. You'd feel cheated if there wasn't one. The funny thing is the cats still here even though he seemed to belong with the boy.

'Is this your cat?' I ask Gran.

'Oh dear is Marley up there he thinks its his room I'm afraid,' I remember a play on television that really was by Dickens about Jacob Marley's ghost. Then Marley opens the door with his paw and goes downstairs and I go to bed. I'm not thinking about the ghost. What I'm thinking was how Charles Dickens would be surprised his stories were on television even though everything else has changed. Very surprised as they didn't have television then but that his stories were still part of it. Which would make them real ghost stories.

Our cat's called Spider. We called her Spider because she caught a spider when we first had her, when she was a kitten. Did Gran and Grandad call their cat Marley because he saw a ghost?

CHAPTER TWO

You know how people say it'll all look different in the morning. They're right, it did. It even sounded different because what I thought might be an old man snoring, Grandad probably, turns out to be a hot air balloon going past my bedroom window and people in a basket with flames spurting up. A fountain of fire, to keep the air hot, I wonder what would happen if the fire went out, it would be worse than running out of petrol. Someone in the balloon basket waves out to me and I wave back which is a surreal beginning for a new day.

Gran says do I want to go to the Zoo or Explore@Bristol. I say, Explore@Bristol though I really want to go to the Zoo but I've been to the Zoo before and going to the Zoo makes it sound like my parents have split up. Also because people might think you like animals being kept in cages which I don't. I mean I prefer them being free but Gran wasn't offering to take me on a Safari holiday.

I didn't know what Explore@Bristol was till we got there. Its a bit like the Millennium Dome. I went to the Dome and if it wasn't for the ghost I'd have written about it though it was a long time ago. Well it was 2000 obviously, which is five years ago and before Ed was ill. He said it was useless but I thought it was brilliant, well when we were there. I was only seven. Ed was interested really, though he made fun of it.

'What's the answer to the meaning of the universe, I know I'll ask a sofa?' : They had talking sofas!

'It's not rocket science,' Dad said.

'No you can't go to the moon for twenty quid,' said Mum.

Grandad seems to like Explore@Bristol which is a modern museum. I mean there aren't any old bones or stones or even boats like at seaside museums and how people used to travel before they had cars. So I shouldn't have thought of the ghost but I did. Gran was looking at how the brain works, it's a model brain that lights up to show which bits you're thinking with and I thought someone like Clocker Wallace would keep using the same bit over and over again. If you were dead the light wouldn't come on at all and a ghost wouldn't be able to think. Grandad was looking at what makes ships sink, you could make a toy ship sink by pressing a button.

'Hardly the Titanic,' Gran shrugs. There weren't any icebergs but there were a lot of buttons. I thought how the ghost boy would be impressed, I knew he wouldn't have toys like this. Some children were playing a game, volleyball I think, on a screen. You just hit the air and a ball moved on the screen. I'd bought a postcard of Saturn to send to Ed and was trying to tell him about it. But I couldn't explain it. I'm not someone who likes to know how things work. Anyway you don't need to know, well only if you're the repair man.

'Go on, have a go.' says Grandad.

I thought I might not be able to hit a ball if it wasn't there because I'm not very good when there is one. Ed would know how it works like he'd know how the magician got a rabbit in his hat and say I was easily impressed. I am. Then I thought if you can hit a ball in the air and make it move on a screen without touching it what was so special about a boy in my room who wasn't really there. I'd only seen him, not played volleyball.

Outside the sun's come out and little children were playing in water and fountains like we were in a another country. Mostly kicking water at each other, it was very shallow but I think it was meant to be ornamental not a paddling pool. There was a baby girl with just a plastic nappy on, like an advert for nappies, she had bright ginger hair and very pale skin, she looked like a baby from a long time ago but I don't suppose they'd have had plastic nappies then, more like towels. A little black girl in a wet T shirt and no pants at all but with lots of sticky out plaits, who looked more modern, ran into her and she fell into a flat wall of water. It looked like a magic wall where you'd come out the other side in Narnia or somewhere. She didn't. She started crying and her mother had to jump in and rescue her. She had ginger hair too.

'Very genetic ginger hair,' says Gran.

'If it's so genetic why aren't there more people with ginger hair?' said Grandad sounding a bit like Ed. I think of red squirrels, how there's not so many as grey ones even though there used to be more.

The woman was very pregnant. Her stomach was stretched over her T-shirt. You could see her belly button sticking out. It made it look like a stopper as though if you pulled it the baby would come out like in Alien. When my cousin Leanne first told me where babies came from I was surprised.

'Where did you think they came from?' she asked. I hadn't. I'd never thought about it at all but it seems obvious now. We are mammals. When me and Sophe saw a baby giraffe being born on a wildlife programme Sophe said if she was a giraffe she'd adopt.

'It looks like the populations about to double,' says Gran as though it's a disaster movie.

'Not unless its twins,' Grandad sounds so like Ed I thought it must be genetic.

Then a dog who'd been in the water came and shook himself all over us.

'Lets find a Pub,' Grandad suggested leading the way. We walked along by the river and there was a bridge with big horns called Pero's bridge. Grandad said Pero was a slave who came to Bristol when people had slaves.

'Did he build it?' I ask. Gran says it was a new bridge, and Pero wasn't a slave, they didn't have slaves in Bristol, Pero was a servant, she'd been to the house where he worked, which was still there. There'd been people dressed up in the clothes of the time acting the parts of the servants like when the house was new. Grandad said it was owned by a man who had slave plantations in America and the merchants from Bristol sent ships out to buy people from Africa to send out to America. It didn't sound possible with black people sitting outside the pubs eating and drinking but things in history always sound unlikely so do things on the news. Anyway this man brought Pero back with him as it was fashionable to have black servants then. I thought of mentioning the ghost again who was in their house wearing the wrong clothes but I didn't. It would sound as though I was making it up because of Pero.

We sat outside a pub by the river, which had a lot of boats on it. We were eating spicy wraps and it felt like being on holiday and I was glad I'd come. Grandad said how all the girls had their bra straps showing.

'Yes but they all match,' says Gran. They did, the ones in black T-shirts had black straps and one's in white T-shirts had white straps except for a girl in a yellow T-shirt who had turquoise straps which Grandad points out triumphantly as though he'd seen a rare butterfly.

'I don't think they're dressing for you,' says Gran.

'I don't expect they even notice I'm here, says Grandad, 'I'm invisible to them.' As we got up to go another group of girls moved onto our table. When I looked back I couldn't see which table we'd been sitting on.

We walked up some steps with the back of a cathedral on one side with iron gates you could look through with gravestones and roses and an old woman sitting on a seat reading a book. On the other side was the back of a hotel where the people who worked there sat on the steps smoking and talking on their mobiles. It looked like two different centuries. If the ghost was here he'd be sitting with the woman in the Cathedral garden.

At the top was a green space with trees and a statue of Queen Victoria and boys on skateboards who'd thrown their trainers into a tree so they hung there like fruit.

'A shoe tree,' Gran looks up to take a photo and nearly gets knocked over by a skateboarder who swerves sharply to avoid her and makes a whooping noise as though Gran was part of an assault course. A hazard.

The front of the cathedral looks like a postcard but we walk the other way down through the town centre which has decking and water jets and two little boys sort of riding on them like seahorses.

'Looks like they're having a pee,' Grandad says. The boys were laughing a lot. I think they were thinking what Grandad was thinking. A statue of Neptune was looking over them like a carer. Grandad says he's going to see a man about a dog which I thought means he wants a pee too.

'Back to the Pub, you mean,' says Gran.

Me and Gran get on a bus to go to Cribbs Causeway. Cribbs Causeway's a shopping mall. Sophe told me to go to it as she'd looked up Bristol shopping malls on the net when I said I was coming here. It's the same as any other shopping mall. Which might be the point of shopping malls and if a Martian came to earth to do some shopping he wouldn't need a map. It's got a fountain, a proper one, a spurty one that jerks up suddenly when we go by like we've stepped on its switch. Like the haunted house in Disneyland when scary things happened as you went by, skeletons climbing out of coffins and proper ghosts. Ed kept saying, 'Its on a sensor.' Perhaps the fountain's on a sensor, or it's gone wrong and about to flood the place. Gran buys me a top that starts blue and then goes green and then bluey green with a white edge. Gran says it looks like the Mediterranean. I think all I need is the Taj Mahal.

She was going on about how she used to go shopping with her sister Jackie when she was a girl. But not in the Mall because it wasn't built then and how her sister had died in 2000 and had never been to the Mall which made her sad because Jackie loved shopping. But it didn't sound very drastic. Not going to the Mall I mean, not dying, which is very drastic. She was sixty when she died, which is quite old, nearly as old as Gran. But it isn't as old as Mrs. Wooley next door who's ninety two and when we went to her ninetieth birthday she made a speech and said she was still learning something new every day. Ed said, 'What for?'

By the time we sit down for a cup of tea Gran says, 'She didn't miss a trick.' Then sighs and says, 'except old age,' she means her sister obviously, she doesn't know Mrs. Wooley, anyway she hasn't missed old age.

I forget all about the ghost boy till I'm going to bed. He doesn't appear so I really believe I've made him up like it might be a hallucination from travelling, road lag or something. Which I haven't heard of, but there probably is such a thing like a lawyer might know about and say, 'My client was suffering from severe road lag at the time and consequently mistook the intruder for a ghost.'

CHAPTER THREE

Next day Grandad was going to work. I was surprised he was going to work. I thought he was too old. He's sixty four which is nearly thirty years younger than Mrs. Wooley, who's still learning something new every day? Gran gave up work last year when she was sixty, as she gets a pension. Grandad has to wait till he's sixty five, though he's a man and men don't usually live as long as women.

'Its not fair,' he says.

'What is?' says Gran and then goes on about all the things that are unfair to women which seems to be quite a lot especially in the past and other countries.

'Will I get a pension when I'm sixty?' I say to shut Gran up. I'm not serious as obviously I can't worry about that yet and as Gran says a lot more things will have changed by then. Grandad says, 'pigs will fly.' Gran says, 'and we'll all look like Anne Robinson.' Which doesn't sound much to look forward to.

Ed would have more interesting ideas. He likes the future. Anyway with Grandad at work that only leaves me and Gran and she can't drive.

'We can go for a walk,' she says as though we're in a book for preschool children. 'Today Matilda went for a walk with Granny, they went to feed the ducks. Quack, Quack, said the ducks as they swan round the pond.' And they'd eat Granny's bread, which was wholemeal of course. On the next page they'd see a fire engine, perhaps the fire engine would have to use the pond to get some water to put out the fire and the ducks would have to walk round the green making sad quacking noises, then it would rain really hard and the pond would fill up. I am quite pleased with this story and I wish I had a little sister to tell it to.

Its not like that. We walk through muddy fields with Gran telling me things she did when she was a girl till she almost seems like a girl. How this was where they picked bluebells. There aren't any bluebells now, not just because they're over but because of the pine trees. The ones they planted when she was a teenager which are now an evergreen wood, a dark, dark wood wood where the light can't get in with wood pigeons cooing in a threatening kind of way like they're putting a spell on you. It was brambles in her day and primrose paths with thrushes and skylarks, birds who could sing.

'Fancy being old enough to see a whole wood grow up,' she says which doesn't sound too bad. I've seen a new road built which seems like an old road already. I've forgotten what it looked like before. There's a cycle track which Gran says is new though it doesn't look new, just muddy tracks over stones, like its always been here. Gran approves of it because she thinks children should get out more. I say we do go abroad more and meet more different people. I know children who've have come from India, Iraq, Pakistan and Somalia, not just next door. There's Samson from Kenya who only started this term he looked like he'd just walked out of one of those television programmes about hungry children and into our class but now he just looks part of it. He is very thin but I think its genetic not hunger. I explain this to Gran who says there was a girl from Scotland in her class who she thought of as foreign because she couldn't understand her accent and she called herself Jeanie instead of Jean. Even worse she called sweets sweeties which Gran thought was babyish but she was actually quite clever and passed the eleven plus.

'When I was your age this was mostly grass eaten short by rabbits and my father and Uncles played golf on a homemade golf course on Sunday afternoons.'

'It was all green fields round here, when I was a girl,' I say in a sing song voice. Gran really is going on.

'Worse things have happened elsewhere,' she says seriously. I think of the war in Iraq and AID's orphans in Africa and the all the people who drowned in the Tsunami. I don't know what Gran thinks of. She must have a lot more to choose from.

Some boys come bouncing over a jump on the cycle path and smatter us with mud and a brown deer that must have been there all the time but I hadn't noticed before, runs away bouncing higher than the cyclists as though he's leaping through an American prairie.

' I s'pose that's what they mean by breaking cover,' says Gran who is impressed too. Its feels quiet after they've gone till Gran gets excited about a bird she says is a bullfinch, its got a pink breast, brighter than a robin but not so friendly. But I feel like I'm on a wildlife programme where unusual birds and rare animals appear all the time as if they're common but really the cameramen have waited all week just to see an otter. Then we come to some men cutting down the trees.

'Oh no,' says Gran, 'I've outlived a wood.'

'That is seriously old, ' I agree.

'What are you cutting them down for?' Gran asks the man with the chainsaw.

'Coffins.' He says and she looks like she's seen a ghost too.

There is a stump of a dead tree in the wood, on a stony bit. 'An Ash tree,' Gran says which they used to climb when she was a girl. I try to think of Gran and her sister climbing the tree in check cotton dresses, but I can't. Not without a photograph.

On a school trip to Paris we went to Versailles where Marie Antoinette lived before she was beheaded. Sophe said, 'Imagine her coming down these stairs and going to have her head chopped off.' I couldn't, even though Sophe started walking like she was wearing a long dress. Gran is saying about children going out to play again. It sounds like a nursery rhyme. 'Jackie and Jenny went out to play and climbed an Ash tree every day.' It was an iron ore mine before she was born apparently, whatever that is? They used to climb down muddy pits into caves where miners used to work. Now they're just shallow dips, more like a skateboard ramp.

'We used to walk across the canyons on tree trunks the gypsies cut down.' She made it sound like an adventure park. I think of gypsies, Gran's gypsies I mean, with painted caravans like in the real museum and spotted scarves on sticks with their dinner in. When I say this to Gran she says, 'Sounds more like Dick Whittington.' Well it is her turn to be sarcastic.

Then she says she lost a dog's lead here and starts looking around as if expecting to find it. I think she means like fifty years ago when she was out to play but she says it was only last year when she was going for a walk with a woman called Linda who had a Labrador Cross called Hollie. It was a leather lead and they couldn't find it in the Autumn leaves so Linda bought her a new yellow one so it would be easy to find next time.

'She's dead now, Hollie.'

So why is she still looking for her lead? No wonder she's got a ghost in her bedroom. Then I see him. My ghost, not the dead dog. He's climbing the tree, it's grown back into a tree like in a speeded up nature film. He's struggling a bit then swinging himself up onto a kind of platform where all the branches came out from the middle. They're thick branches, the tree was old even then.

I look at Gran to see if she could see him. But she doesn't look like she could so I don't s ask. It was like she wasn't there. Like only the boy was and this was happening in a different time zone. Ed might have name for it, a fourth dimension perhaps which is something else I'm not sure what it is. I don't even know what a third dimension is. Not something I'd want an exam question about. I wish I'd watched more sci-fi stuff or even Dr. Who. I'm probably in a time loop. Is there such a thing? I mean is it something scientist might know about or something made up like a cyber man.

There's a dog sat at the bottom of the tree and grass and bluebells. I go forward to stroke the dog, a brown spaniel with shiny fur and a dribbly mouth but as I get closer it disappears. I couldn't see the boy anymore either so I wasn't sure if he was my boy or if the place was riddled with ghosts and phantoms like I'd walked into a phantom area. That is was particularly haunted like when people dig up old Roman coins and when they find one they find a lot.

'Be careful,' said Gran and I could see I was in the middle of a bramble bush. It was today's brambles. Perhaps I'd stepped on a crack in time, invaded the past and nothing would be the same again?

Gran is saying about a big tree falling down right where we're standing and I get a scary feeling as though it fell on someone and killed them and that's why my ghost is here. But she goes on about how they played on the fallen tree and her Dad collected logs and how much they got out of it even if you didn't count the insects and fungi and so it stops sounding like a killer tree more like environmental studies.

'Sorry I'm boring you going on about my childhood, my Grandma used to tell me about hers, I thought I'll never do that when I have grandchildren, but here I am,' she says as though she doesn't have any choice like having to wear glasses.

We walk along a path which Gran said they used to call the green path. It isn't green anymore, it's brown with dead pine needles. There's a noise from a tree and we both jump but it's only another wood pigeon making more noise than you'd imagine a pigeon being able to make.

'Look,' she says and there's a little mouse hurrying around not noticing us as he's only interested in mouse things, and I think if Gran can see a mouse she'd hardly have missed a boy and a dog.

When we get back to our road, I think of it as our road already, there's a girl on a horse.

'Hello Failand, this is my grand daughter Matilda,' says Gran. I'd never met anyone called Failand before though I know an India and a Chelsea. There is a place up the road from here called Failand, its on the signpost, so perhaps it wasn't so amazing. Anyway I'm thinking about this and I realise Gran has asked Failand if I can go out with her tomorrow. She lives next door to Gran. I feel embarrassed but Failand sounds friendly in a way posh people have of sounding friendly even if they don't feel it. Well not so much posh as confident, it makes them sound like they know everything. Izzie Russell in our class sounds clever because she talks posh, but she isn't particularly even though her Mum's a Doctor. But I don't suppose that's her fault. Some children say she's putting it on but I think she'd be putting it on if she spoke rough.

Failand is saying, 'Goodbye Jenny,' to Gran which I don't like because it makes her sound more her friend than my Gran. I call Mrs. Wooley next door Mavis and she's about Gran's age but I call old Mrs. Wooley, who is Mavis's mother, Mrs. Wolley though her name is Violet. Sophe calls her Vi.

I tell Gran I can't ride, she says she can't drive but that doesn't stop her getting a lift. I try to say you can't have a lift on a horse, well only in cowboy films or olden days.

After tea Gran gets out a photograph album which is full of olden days with black and white photos. There's one of her Mum and Dad, my great grandparents, Len and Elsie sat on deckchairs on a beach not looking as old fashioned as you would expect. Len's wearing a white shirt and smoking a cigarette. I can't remember him, he died of lung cancer before I was born. There's one of Grandad about seven, with glasses on, sat on a doorstep with his sister Pat which looks older but must be the same time, perhaps it's the doorstep or because his sisters got a big floppy bow of ribbon in her hair. There's one of Gran and Grandad getting married with her sister Jackie and Grandad's sister Pat, now more grown up, as bridesmaids. The bridesmaids are wearing big bows too. They aren't in order. There's lots of pictures of my Dad when he was a little boy, followed by a picture of Gran when she was a little girl holding her mother's hand in the garden, this garden but with the apple tree very small and her sister Jackie with plaits holding a cat. In the background is a pram, a big pram like you'd expect a Nanny to push in a park in London when Prince Charles was a baby. Grandad has noticed they're not in order too and says they ought to go on the computer and be catalogued.

He's got lots of photos on the computer already that come up at random like a moving screensaver, coloured ones of hot air balloons and wild flowers and trees taken by Gran. There's Bristol suspension bridge in the snow and foreign towns and pale beaches taken on their holidays. There's me Mum, Dad and Ed sat in the garden the last time we came here. But mostly Marley the cat, sat on the mat and on the windowsill and on the bed and out in the garden. Even Marley the kitten.

'The most photographed cat in the world,' says Grandad.

'I wouldn't bet on it,' says Gran.

Then she says he can't put the old photos on the computer because they weren't taken with a digital camera. Grandad says a computer can do anything if you know what keys to press.

'Ah there's the rub,' says Gran which I don't get. But afterwards think she meant knowing what keys to press. By now Grandad is singing. 'I've go the whole world in my hands,' which I suppose is an old song. But Grandad likes computers almost as much as Ed but for different things. He's on an Ancestor website.

'It's a minefield out there.'

'I thought you came of farming stock?' says Gran though he meant the internet was a minefield, not that his ancestors were coal miners. Gran knew that of course. He's found an old ancestor called John who got sent to prison for poaching.

'Was he hung for a sheep or a lamb?' asks Gran.

'Who's in the pram?' I want to know because no one's mentioned a baby before.

'My brother, Christopher, he died when he was young,' she says sharply like she doesn't want to talk about it. I expect he died when he was a baby, more babies died then, though it wasn't Victorian times, more war time, World War II, 1939-1945 it says on the war memorial where me and Sophe sit and read the names and choose a fantasy boyfriend. Sophe's chosen Walter Postlewaite because she thinks that's the worst name. I've chosen James Winter, which I think is the best, it's the last, because they're in alphabetical order not because he was the last to die. More like calling the register. Now I think Walt and Jim as we call them might still have been alive when some of these photo's were taken. I've never thought of them as real people before. All the people in the photo in the garden are dead, and the cat of course, except for my Gran. They could be on a war memorial or a Pub wall like an old cricket team. I mention the War and Gran says she can't remember. Grandad who is scanning the old photo's says he can just about remember a Victory party in the street where he lived. Gran says she can remember getting a coronation mug. The war would have been over by then and Jim and Walt just names even if they are written in stone.

'Did you have a dog when you were little?' I ask remembering the dog in the field.

'Yes, a spaniel, Joe,' she sounds surprised. I think she must wonder how I knew but then I hadn't said it was spaniel or I'd seen his ghost. Just a dog, anyone could have a dog.

Granddad says they had a budgie called Joey, a green one and all budgerigars were green originally.

'And they were all called Joey,' says Gran.

When I go to bed the ghost boy is sat on the bed reading a book. I say, 'Hello.' I don't expect him to answer anymore than I expect Jim and Walt to answer when Sophe says, 'Going down the King's Head tonight boys, they've got a quiz but don't go a joker on the pop music round.'

Then he says, 'Hello,' the boy, not James Winter. Or I think he does. I wonder if its some kind of trick, a recording, or if my Grandad is a secret ventriloquist and he's going to come out of the wardrobe and start laughing which would be really scary, more scary than having a ghost in your bedroom. I had a teddy once who talked when you pulled his string, he said teddy bear things like, 'I want some honey. I feel very sleepy. I want to go to bed.' I want to say, 'Who's pulling your strings,' to the ghost but I don't because he'll think I'm calling him a puppet.

'What are you doing here?' he asks me which seems a nerve but then I think he may have been here first. So I start telling him about coming here and Ed being ill and everything. I think if people at school could see me talking to an apparition I'd be on Facebook. Then I feel a worried like someone is watching us, like I was shoplifting and there was CCTV. But there's only me and him and he feels familiar now, I've even got used to his clothes. He asks me my name and I think now would be a good time to start calling myself Tilly but it doesn't seem important so I say Matilda which I hardly ever say.

'What's yours?'

'Christopher.' Yes I'm actually asking. And he actually answers. Its like we're playing the volley ball game in Explore@Bristol.

I remember Gran's dead baby brother. Could this be him or just a coincidence? He's not a baby. I think of Ed and wonder if this is an omen. What if he's dead and is trying to come and see me, like people say happens when people die. Sophe said the day her Grandad died she had an omen though she didn't say what it was. I remember my other Gran, my Mum's mother saying how she saw her Dad walking upstairs after she came back from the funeral. Maybe its hereditary. But if Ed was trying to contact me he wouldn't call himself Christopher, well he'd have shortened it to Chris at least. Unless he inhabited Christopher's body, but Christopher hasn't got a body. Only an image. I'm scaring myself. I don't want to think about Ed being dead and getting mixed up with this boy who died ages ago. You know on gravestones how when someone who died in 2000, when they were a hundred say, about being reunited with their husband who died in 1960 when they were young. I mean they wouldn't recognise each other. Well the person who died last would but not the one who died first. I mean if it was Christopher, Gran's brother, he wouldn't recognise Gran, an old lady, who he'd only known as a girl who climbed trees but she'd know him because he'd still be the same. That's if there is an afterlife of course, which I find hard to believe but lots of people do. Which I find hard to believe as well, lots of people believing I mean, though its hard to think there isn't anywhere, that you just disappear. Rubbish doesn't disappear just because you've put it in the dustbin, even if it doesn't get recycled it goes into landfill or even if it gets burnt there's carbon and stuff. I think we must go somewhere too. I don't know where. It would mean inventing a new religion.

When they say joined in holy matrimony which Sophe says is an old way of saying having sex but I think they mean joined by God. A faith thing, as though he was there joining them, in the name of the father. When I was a bridesmaid for Leanne, my cousin, I didn't feel that God was there, joining them up, even though it was a church wedding. I was wearing a pale pink dress from Monsoon, another girl who I didn't know was wearing pale blue one, and Annabel another cousin was wearing a yellow one we were supposed to look like flowers but we didn't really. The church had a stained glass window with Jesus carrying a lamb and being a good shepherd. But he didn't feel there, not even in spirit, well not there like Christopher is here. I don't feel afraid of Christopher. More like going round an old house where they've got all the pictures of the ancestors on the wall.

'That's Lord Henry who was killed falling off his horse in 1841,' says the guide almost as if he knew him and he's probably said it so many times he thinks he does. Half the people in films or on telly are dead. Some are only just dead because when they die they show you a series they've been in or an interview they had last year and they look the same. It's the only way you ever knew them, a policeman in The Bill or a barmaid in a sitcom, so it doesn't seem to make any difference them being dead, well not to you.

I'm thinking this and Christopher isn't there any more and I go to bed and dream I'm riding on a horse and I fall off and Ed is saying its all to do with gravity like the man who discovered gravity by watching an apple fall off a tree. I don't know why that means he discovered it, just gave it a name, everybody knows things fall down. Then I wake up and I can hear a horse going by and I wonder what century I'm in. Not that we haven't got horses in Yorkshire but they don't go by our house. It must be Failand. Why doesn't she just call herself Fay. That's what Sophe would call her. I wish Sophe was here. I don't want to ride a horse. She'd say, 'just say no,' like if someone was asking me take drugs. I think I'd sooner take drugs.

CHAPTER FOUR

I go round to Failand's house hoping she's forgotten me. Their house doesn't look the same as Gran and Grandads even on the outside though they're semi detached. What is mostly hedge and pink roses and lavender with bee's on it and things growing up the wall in our garden is mostly driveway and they've got a car parked on it. Grandad's garden path barely has room for a bike. He parks his car in the road.

Also Failand's is totally different inside. Its paler, with less walls but with bigger pictures on them, modern pictures and wooden floors and wide windows. Its much lighter and doesn't look like its the other half of Gran and Grandad's house. It looks like it's in another age despite being in the same road. The kitchen feels twice as big.

It is nearly twice as big because they've built a piece onto it with French windows. Gran and Grandad's house couldn't look like this even if it had a makeover? I'm not sure they'd want it to. One thing I don't think they've got is a ghost in the bedroom. I wonder if that's why Christopher's come back, because its stayed the same. I say this to a woman I think is Failand's Mum, not about Christopher, I don't want to make him sound like a water feature, only how different their house looks. Failand says it's not her Mum, its Maria, she looks after the house and her brother.

'Is she an au pair?' I'de never met anyone with an au pair before.

'She's Maria,' Failand said sharply making it sound like I've said the wrong thing. I think she might be Polish because she's got a foreign accent and fair hair. I don't ask.

I'd better describe Failand who is taller than me with longish brown hair in a pony tail, it curves down in an easy way like a girl in an American film getting into an open car. I wish mine would, which it won't because it's completely straight but not flat like a models. When I try to tie it back it sticks up, more like a horse tail, a horse about to go for a poo. Also Failand's got a longer neck to hang it on. She's got a longer face too. I'm not saying she looks horsey or anything though Sophe might. She's got a brace on her teeth but she smiles quite confidently. It doesn't bother her. She's just wearing an old navy sweatshirt and jeans. I think I'm prettier, but she looks more right somehow. Like if people were looking for a model they'd choose her. Well if they were modelling girls who ride horses.

A boy with blue eyes and blonde hair comes up and stares at me without speaking and I remember one of Ed's old film videos where all the children were blonde and stared at you. It was called The Village of the Damned. I say this to Failand.

'Are you calling him a midwitch cuckoo, that's a first?' but she laughs. She must have seen the film too because that's what they were called, the blonde children who turned out to be aliens. I think I may have said the wrong thing again like I'm calling him an alien. I ask him his name but he doesn't answer. Perhaps he's Maria's son and dosn't speak English. But Failand says, 'My little brother.' Perhaps he's deaf and dumb, I think of saying, 'Has he got hearing difficulties?' but that would make him sound like an old person. I shut up too.

Dad once said, 'Soon nobody will talk to anybody because they keep changing the rules .' but Ed said, 'You've got to keep up.' I want to say about Ed to Failand but I don't because it would be like saying I've got a brother with something wrong with him too as though it was a competition. Anyway it's like totally different.

Then she says, 'Ham's on another planet.' I think she's a vegetarian and talking about not eating meat then I realise she means her brother. I wonder why he's called Ham. There was Ham, Shem and Japhet, Noah's children who were on the arc in the

Bible. Lots of names come from the bible and there's an old watch shop near us with Noah Feinstein written above it. Well it's all boarded up but the name's still there. There's even a picture of an old fashioned man with glasses bending over a watch I used to think it was Noah himself, Noah Feinstein I mean not someone out of the Arc. Now I think its just a picture of a watchmaker. I think it would be better to be called Noah than Ham. I want to call Sophe and say how one's called after a signpost and the other after a sandwich. Sophe's Hamster was always called Hammy till he died and we buried him with a big stone she made her Mum buy from a garden centre and she carved Travis on it.

'Why have you got Travis on his stone?' I asked.

'Because that's his name,' she said. But we always called it Hammy's grave.

We go to see the horse who smells of horse. I recognise it like someone who's used to horses. Like people saying how you'll know how it feels to be in love when you are.

'What's his name?'

'Billy,' and I'm glad he's got an ordinary name though she spoils it by saying it was King William when we bought him but it sounded like a Pub so we call him Billy.

'You can call me Fay by the way, most people do,' but its too late. Anyway I've come round to Failand. We spend a lot of time brushing Billy and though I'd been afraid she'd expect me to know how to ride, now I feel I want to, but she doesn't suggest it. I like being there with the horse. A blackbird with a bright yellow beak comes down to drink from Billy's bucket and we sit on squares of straw like we're in a picture on a calendar. A Calendar like you'd get from a National Trust place, two girls with a horse and a bird on a bucket, August 1950.

Failand seems very efficient, cleaning the stable and I don't really want to clear up horse dung though it doesn't smell too bad not like cats or dogs. I say this to Failand who says its because horses don't eat meat and it makes sense. Sometimes I do think I ought to be a vegetarian but not just to have better smelling poo of course.

When we go back to the house Failand's mother is home.

'I'm Nina, have you met Hamish?' she asks. I say no, but Failand says I have and I realize Ham is Hamish or Hamish is Ham.

'People don't usually forget meeting Hamish.' She laughs. At this point Hamish is shouting about something he's lost, he's making a lot of fuss. Failand goes and finds it for him, it's a piece of Lego. Nobody tells him off. Either he's very spoilt or he's got that shouting disease, like a boy on television. Tourettes, which Ed accuses me of having when I get upset. Nina asks me to stay for tea but I say I'd better go back.

'Do you want to go riding tomorrow?' says Failand.

'I can't ride,' I say but she says everyone should ride, like swimming and she'll get me a horse as if a horse was a packet of crisps. I don't say I can't swim either. I don't know why I can't swim perhaps there's something wrong with me like Hamish, which I havn't figured out yet, or like Gran not being able to drive.

I notice a boy walking up the drive about Ed's age, which is fourteen.

'Is Mum back?' he asks so I know he's another brother.

'Who's your friend?'

'This is Matty.'

'Hi Matty, I'm Miles but you can call me Kilos.'

'Hello Kilos,' which sounds Spanish, he doesn't look Spanish, he's tall with floppy fair hair but not as fair as Ham. He has a nice way of talking, friendly but not embarrassing.

'Its what they call him at school. Miles, kilometres, Kilos,' says Failand and I'm glad she's told me because I don't think I'd have worked it out.

Another girl goes by on a horse 'Kate,' Failand calls and seems to forget me and I'm quite glad. I don't want to meet anyone else which is just as well as Kate doesn't notice I'm there. Though I haven't spoken to her I don't like her which I know isn't fair.

'You shouldn't judge anyone till you've walked a mile in their procession.' It said on a lavatory wall once. I wouldn't mind walking a mile in Miles procession.

Kate's mobile rings and she answers it saying 'I'm on the horse.' I'd like to ring Sophe and say. 'I'm on the horse.' When I get in I ring her anyway but Luce answers and says Sophe's gone out with Aisha.

I feel Sophe has deserted me even though I'm the one who went away. Gran is talking to a woman called Wendy and seems surprised to see me as if she's forgotten I'm staying with her. Neither of them offer me a piece of the cake they're eating. Grandad's playing a card game on the computer. The cat's asleep on the chair facing the telly. The news is on and there's soldiers and tanks and dead bodies, it's breaking news, I mean its really happening and happening now and they're really dead, not just on telly. But no one's watching so it doesn't feel real. I go upstairs. I've forgotten the ghost so I'm surprised to see him. I think what's happening now, those people dying in Iraq hadn't happened when he was alive. They hadn't even been born and now they're dead too. I feel like a time traveller I want to say I know how it feels to be a ghost. I don't because I don't want Christopher to think I'm saying being dead isn't serious.

'What are you doing here?' I say instead though I know he was probably here before I was born but I still feel it's my room now. If all the dead came back there wouldn't be a room big enough? He says, 'I can't choose where I am.' I suppose I'm being really rude like telling a refugee to go back to where they came from. Though this is where he did come from. When he says, 'pick a car.' I choose a green lorry with an open back. When I went to a museum of transport with Grandad he went on about how he used to ride in the back of his Uncle's lorry to Weston when he was a boy and what a treat it was then.

I wondered if Christopher ever went with him in the back of the lorry. But I don't suppose he'd have known him, I mean if Christopher is Gran's brother it doesn't mean Grandad would have known him when he was a boy. Unless Grandad was the boy next door. I don't know why I'm thinking that. Maybe I've sort of regressed and I'm thinking in their language. Like when you're watching an old film on telly and nobody ever goes to work and they only get any money when somebody dies and leaves it to them. I suppose that's why they murder them so often. And I want the murderer to get found out even though I know they'll get hung which I wouldn't want to happen today.

Christopher wants to play this game where we race the cars. I see the green lorry was a bad choice. He's got a red sports car that wins every time. But I feel I'm stuck with it like Dad does with his lottery numbers, though he's not really. I mean there's others to choose from. Christopher already knows the red sports car is the fastest. I think of Ed. I want to tell him about the cars. Then I think they don't even exist. What am I doing here?

'Telephone Matilda,' calls Gran from downstairs and I think its Sophe but I hope its Ed on his mobile from hospital if you're allowed mobiles in hospital because I feel like telling him I've got a ghost in my bedroom. I can't tell Sophe, she'll think I'm so desperate for a boyfriend I've had to make one up. But I wouldn't have made up someone who wore thick trousers and played with toy cars. Would I?

Its Mum, who asks me how I am and sounds like a stranger at first, well not like someone you can tell about a ghost, it will look like I'm scared or completely lost it and anyway Gran might hear. I tell her about Failand and the horse and she sounds all pleased and says, 'I'm glad you've made a friend.' as though I didn't have any friends before. I ask about Ed who she says is doing very well which doesn't mean a lot. But I don't like to ask anymore in case she tells me something I don't want to know. Marley the cat pushes against my legs and I remember him watching the cars go down the ramp and even putting his paw out which means he must have seen them even though they were ghost toys. Perhaps he's on his ninth life so he can see into the past.

'Are you there?' says Mum.

I want to say, 'Are you?' After all she's only a voice. I think of the people falling out of the twin towers when they were blown up and sending their phone messages back and maybe hitting the ground before the other person could answer. Or sending a postcard from their holiday before the Tsunami saying they were having a wonderful time and by the time the person got it they were drowned. I wonder how long I could hold onto a palm tree for because I can't hold on to the bars at Gym for very long. Mum is saying about being careful, on the horse I mean. I ask about Spider though I've hardly thought of Spider, then she says wants she want to talk to Gran. I hear Gran saying, 'You're alright with that then?' and I think she means the horse riding and I wish Mum would say I wasn't allowed to ride, that I'm allergic to horsehair. But they might have been talking about something completely different.

Grandad comes back from the Pub and we have a proper meal, like meat and gravy and cabbage and roast potatoes and I think this is what the ghost boy would have eaten but then we have yoghurt, which spoils it. I want a gooseberry pie or something my

Grandad grew and my Gran cooked. They offer to play scrabble like they're trying to be proper grandparents, which they are and don't have to prove it, we do play even though I can see Gran's missing Coronation Street. So am I. Grandad wins. He takes it very seriously, I think of the boy and his toy cars. Perhaps it's genetic, but it isn't Grandad's brother. Perhaps it's a male thing? I'm not sure. Ella a girl in our class said there isn't any difference between boys and girls except biological ones.

Sophe said, 'Ella wants to get out more.'

Christopher, I'm going to call him Christopher from now on, not ghost boy, is gone when I go to bed. I find some old books in the cupboard I start reading one. Its called Jandy Mac Comes Back, which I think is quite a good name. Jandy Mac is riding a horse and used to go to a school called the Chalet School. She's riding back to see her old friends. It must be a sequel. I think of Failand riding back here in the future but I can't think what it will be like. Anyway I won't even be here this September. When Gran comes up she says it was her book when she was young but she'd forgotten it. She says there was a whole series of books about the Chalet School so it sounds like Hogwarts. I don't think I'd like to read the whole series. I said I liked it though it was old fashioned.

'Everything is in this house, its like living in a time warp, even today's papers seem out of date,' says Gran and I wonder if she knows about Christopher's ghost and is testing me. I want to say I've seen him. I hesitate a bit then say, 'Gran… your brother, Christopher, what did he die of?'

She goes all serious and says, I'm not to worry about Edmund, he'll be alright, they've nearly cracked leukaemia now, but she says it likes she is worried, worried about Ed I mean, not Christopher. I s'pose it's a bit late for that. Then I think perhaps he died of leukaemia and its hereditary. What if Ed did die, I don't think I could stand it and then I think Gran's brother did die and it must have been awful for her and Ed is her grandson. I decide not to say anything about having the ghost of her brother in my bedroom. I almost stop believing in him myself. I mean he can't really exist, it's just some kind of mental illness. Like long dead relatives appearance syndrome. I expect you could look it up on the net or in a medical library. If you had the right name for it: if they took me to a phsychiatrist, he'd say, 'D.R.A.S.' Dead Relative Appearance Syndrome, its quite common at this age,' and give me some tablets and say come back next week if he hasn't disappeared by then.

Gran picks up a car, it's the pick up truck. 'Where did you find this dinky toy?' she says sharply, then, 'Oh it must have been in the cupboard with the books, my brother was always playing with them, I never had the heart to throw them away, its so long since,' she hesitates and I want her to say, since he died and tell me about it but she just says, 'since I looked in that cupboard.' Then I think how she's probably thinking of him now playing with his cars. She can see Christopher just by remembering him, he doesn't have to be a ghost because he's still in living memory.

I've heard of dinky toys but I've never really known what they are. Did the car being real make Christopher more real or less? I mean might he turn up after all like a lost toy, like one kept in a Museum. Like this really was Pooh Bear, not just a copy. Perhaps he'd been kidnapped and taken abroad, missing believed dead. I try to imagine him knocking at the door at Christmas. White haired but sun tanned, wearing an expensive suit, with an American accent saying "Hi sis it's been a long time, a helluva long time." Ed would record it on video.

When I go to sleep I dream I'm in a quiz and my question is, 'What's a Dinky toy?' and I say 'Small model cars popular in the 1950's.' and Ed says, 'Nice one sis' though he's never called me sis in real life. Clocker Wallace is in the quiz and I think he won't know anything but someone asks him what time it was when Marie Antoinette got beheaded and he says, 'Its late, its late,' like Alice's white rabbit. I wake up thinking of Marie Antoinette coming down the stone steps in a long dress going to get beheaded.

CHAPTER FIVE

Failand rings early to say she can't get me a horse but she'll get me one on Saturday and we'll go to Ashton Court. I'm disappointed, though I didn't think I wanted one and I didn't really believe there'd be one. But a part of me did, a part of me could see myself in a cowboy film galloping across the plains. One where the man meets a woman who can ride as fast as him but when they stop the woman pushes back her hat and her hair falls down all blonde and wavy and the man looks at her like he's only just noticed her and how pretty she is. I knew it wouldn't have been like that but I go and wash my hair anyway.

'A horse, a horse my kingdom for a horse,' says Grandad unexpectedly when I explain.

'Richard II,' says Gran like she's in school.

'No, Richard III.' They are in the pub quiz team. I s'pose it keeps their minds active, like going to the brain gym.

Then he says, 'Come on I'll take you to Clevedon, there's plenty of horses on the Failand road, its Gymkhana Street up there.' I'm expecting to go to a horse show but Clevedon's a beach. Well its an estuary not a sea. You can see Wales. They've got a pier which fell down and has been put together again. Of course Gran can remember the old one, well it's the same one. She says how it was left for ages in pieces like a giant Meccano set.

'What's a Meccano set?' I say.

'Metal Lego,' says Grandad.

We go to the amusement arcade which isn't an arcade exactly, more a machine hut, but I am not amused as Queen Victoria said. I don't know what about, not Clevedon's Amusement Arcade anyway. Though this is a Victorian town which is probably why I'm thinking about what she said. I am a ghost whisperer after all. We go for a walk called Poets Walk. Alfred Tennyson who was a Victorian poet stayed here. He had a friend called Hallam who used to live in a big house which is still here too but he drowned at sea and his body was brought back and buried in the churchyard on the hill. Tennyson wrote a poem about it. I think Hallam's a nice name for a boy. In the church there's a tombstone. Hallam was the surname, his first name was Arthur. The whole Hallam family is buried here and it looks like a lot of them died young so perhaps Arthur's death wasn't such a shock. And Tennyson wrote a lot of poems. There's a plaque for two boys who drowned ages ago near Weston. Gran says a girl drowned in the same place this year and I think drowning is something that hasn't changed, as a way of dying I mean. Is it how Christopher died?

There's a lot of graves in the churchyard too. Its like it belongs to dead people, like we shouldn't be here. Well not till we qualify by being dead ourselves. We stop to read some names of people who've died recently they've only got little stones not like the old graves. But they have got fresh flowers, a butterfly lands on one, the stone not the flower.

'A Red Admiral, I suppose he just wants to warm his wings up,' says Gran all pleased. I suppose they've been cremated so there isn't so much left to bury. I wonder if Christopher was cremated or if he's just old bones by now. How long does it take to turn into a skeleton?

I wonder what people mean when they say someone's remains have been found. Someone who's been murdered years ago and they can only tell who it is by their teeth.

Well their dental records. I wonder what remains of Christopher and if he's buried in this churchyard. I don't ask.

'O look their mother's gone now,' Gran's bending over a grave and I think it's someone she knew when they were alive. It's a stone like an open book with two names, Steven and Sarah, a brother and sister, on the first page. Taken tragically it says. A car accident Gran thinks and now their Mum has died, twenty years later.

'There were always fresh flowers. To think of her coming here all these years and now she's here too.' Gran says sadly. It is a sad story.

   I remember the McDonalds, these three boys who lived near us who were like "the bad family," not really bad like gun crime or drugs more stealing cars. One day I was going home alone after a row with Sophe and they were blocking the pavement working on an old car. I was a bit scared to go past them. One of them said, 'She's scared.'
Then another one said. 'Gangway lads let the lady go by, don't worry about them Mattie they're soft as shit.' He knew my name? Not long after that he was killed joyriding in a stolen car. Andy his name was, there were all these flowers on the railings, it was near our school and there was a photo of him looking like he was in a boy band. But some people said he deserved it, that the family had it coming. But you wouldn't hang a person for stealing a car, I suppose they might have once when you got hung for stealing a sheep, I mean if they'd had cars then. His brother only broke his leg and he was out driving again pretty soon. I felt I knew him when he died as though he'd been my friend and I wanted to put some flowers on the railings and say from Mattie but I never did.

'More dead than alive,' says Grandad and I don't know if he means the place or the people. A shrew runs across a stone which says Robert (Bob) Webb. Much loved father and grandfather. He was born in 1952.

38

'Younger than us,' says Gran.

'The year the king died,' says Grandad and goes on about how he was at school and the teacher came in to say; The King is dead. How it sounded like a history lesson even then and now it is. Outside there's five donkeys looking over a gate and a woman in a long skirt comes to feed them with carrots. I told you everything that happens here could have happened a hundred years ago.

We have a meal in a Pub with pictures of old Clevedon, people walking along the sea front in long dresses, which looks the same, the sea front I mean, not the dresses. I win five pounds on the machine and Grandad says he knows a better Pub. He certainly knows a lot. We go past a very bent over tree by a bandstand. There's actually a band, a Salvation Army band playing on the bandstand. Then a very bent old woman goes under the very bent old tree and Grandad says, 'That just about sums up Clevedon.'

Grans gets her camera out to take a photo but by the time she's turned it on the old woman's gone past the tree.

We go to the other Pub which Grandad says, 'Looks like Bates's Motel in Psycho,' Psycho's an old film where a woman gets murdered in a shower by a man who keeps his dead mother in a chair. In case you haven't seen it. I saw it on a video with Ed. He collects old films. It's very scary and this Pub does look like the hotel from the outside, probably because its Victorian and they had a lot of murders then. I think. More poison than gun crime, which seems creepier. Well it takes longer.

It's opposite the pier, which isn't an amusement Pier more a boat Pier which is what I think Piers were meant to be. Gran says there is a boat called the Waverley which is the oldest paddle steamer. I don't know if she means in the World or in Clevedon? I want to tell Ed. I buy a postcard of the bandstand and the very bent over tree and say about the bent old woman walking under it and what Grandad said because I think he'll like it. There's a bit of space left. I feel I ought to mention his illness but I don't want to. I just say. 'I'm writing this in a replica of Bates Motel, dare I go to the toilet?'

There's a man playing a guitar and the sun is setting, silver at first making a shining path in the sea with a little yacht going through it, I wonder if its silver for them or only us. You know how things look different when you're in them. The Waverley comes in to the pier and I can see people get off and walk along the pier to their cars and the sun is going down, big and round and heavy looking like a red hot canon ball as though it'll sink when it reaches the sea. I think of it lying at the bottom of the sea and the sea bubbling up with the heat and cooking the fish and spilling out all over the world. You could make an animation film. Ed would say, we've got the technology. But I wouldn't know how to use it.

We lean over the railings for a bit to watch the sunset and the tide is in against the wall except for a bit of concrete by the pier where some people are having a barbecue. Not a proper one just foil cartons with flames coming out of them, they're dancing and it looks a bit pagan. I wish I had some more room on my postcard. I look for Christopher but he isn't here. Children are throwing stones into the sea. The children all look modern. I wonder if any of them are the great, great grandchildren of the people in the pictures on the Pub wall but I don't really think they are. They don't look related to the ones in the pictures even though they probably did throw pebbles into the sea but maybe not on a Sunday. Though perhaps Robert who had a shrew run over his gravestone was their beloved Grandad. Two Asian girls in pink and orange saris run down the steps and I suppose their great grandparents would have lived in India, which takes us back to Queen Victoria. I don't really want to go there but I am bewitched.

I post my card in a post box in the wall between the Psycho Pub and some Gents toilets that must have been there when the Victorians were here. If Sophe was here she'd make something up about Victorian men going to the toilet and having to undo their buttons because zips wouldn't have been invented. The tide is coming right over the wall when we get back in the car, there's seaweed on the pavement, someone's collecting it in a black paper sack. Whatever for? We go past the big old houses where the windows are lit up and you can see people inside watching television.

'It looks so depressing,' says Grandad.

'Yes I expect they're all occupied by old women waiting to die,' says Grandad and there is an old lady looking out of window like a traditional ghost.

'But they were new once and she was young.' says Gran.

'And her brother died in the war and her sister died of consumption, the one who could play the piano so well,' said Grandad, not sounding like Grandad like he's under the spell too. And he laughs but rather maliciously and I wish he hadn't said that because it made me think of Ed and I think Gran might be thinking of Christopher. Maybe he died of consumption but it wasn't that long ago. Maybe he was the last to die of it.

'What's Consumption?'

Gran says its what they used to call TB which I have heard of, its something cows get, they catch it from badgers. Then we actually see a badger and Gran and Grandad get very excited as though they hadn't seen a badger before. Well not a live one. Not that I have, well not a wild one crossing the road in the dark. I wonder if it's got TB.

When we get back I go straight to bed. Christopher is there even though it's late and I'm not in the mood. I know late is when you'd expect to see a ghost, he didn't feel like a ghost. More like a friend, you know how a friend can turn up when you don't want them to and not turn up when you really want them. He didn't have his cars but a construction game and I remembered Grandad saying metal Lego.

'What's that?'

'A crane,' which was what he was making not what it was. It looked like the only thing you could make with it except the Eiffel Tower. I asked again and he said, 'Meccano.' I asked about Clevedon and the pier to test him and he said he'd been on the pier which means he must date back to before the pier fell down though I've forgotten when that was. Also I've had another thought which I think is quite clever. Its about people who've got something wrong with them like Clocker Wallace or Ham or very old people forgetting things like bits of their brain have worn out or even cows with BSE who's brains are a real mess. What if I've got an extra bit, a bit that lets me see people who aren't here anymore. I don't mean I'm extra clever or anything. I mean it might not be a good thing, like having an extra finger wouldn't be a good thing. More like you were a bit deformed and if you'd lived in the middle ages or somewhere where they didn't understand disability they'd think you were a witch. I want to say this to Ed. He isn't here, Christopher is. I ask him.

'If you had an extra finger would you want to have it off even it was useful. He says he doesn't think it would be very handy or we'd all have six fingers to start with.

I say but it would be very HANDY and we both start laughing so much that Gran comes up and asks what's the matter. I ask her if she had an extra finger would she want to keep it in case it came in handy. She thinks this is supposed to be a joke too but she doesn't laugh. Of course she doesn't notice Christopher as she hasn't got the extra bit of brain and I can't see him anymore so I suppose my extra bit of brain isn't lit up. I think of

Marley watching the dinky cars and I suppose he'd have an extra bit of brain too. A psychic cat? I like it.

I go to bed and dream of the dead woman before she was dead taking flowers to the grave of her dead children and falling in and she cries out, 'They're not here.' I'm riding by on a horse but I don't stop to pull her out in case I fall in too.

'The horse wouldn't stop,' I say when I get back and it turns out the woman in the grave is Princess Diana. I wonder if that's because of the picture of Diana by the Taj Mahal, which is a grave. Or because she's dead herself and her grave is on an island and people who didn't know her cried when she died which Ed said was hysteria. Or was it like Gran knowing the dead people of Clevedon even though she didn't know them except through their gravestones. People knew Diana from being on television so much. And Sophe could imagine Marie Antoinette walking down the steps to be beheaded who'd been dead before television was invented.

CHAPTER SIX

On Saturday I really am riding a horse. We clip clop along like the start of a cowboy film. Well its Ridgeway road which isn't at all like cowboy country more like an old fashioned film. The houses get bigger and bigger with verandas, old veranda's I mean like they had servants and gardeners and everyone rode horses. Though its cars in the driveways. I expect its stables round the back. I say this to Failand who says it used to be old tennis courts now its new houses. We turn off and go down a steep hill which is the scariest bit of all I keep thinking my horse is going to slip, sometimes it does little slips and I don't talk anymore. I feel sick. I want to get off but I'm too high up to get down and its like knowing the big wheel won't stop just for you, you have to wait to the end of the ride. A car comes by and my horse rears up a bit and the man driving says something about you ought to have a licence for that, but he does slow down so I'm grateful. Kate turns round and tells him I'm a novice rider, and he should respect that. But I agree with the man. Gran shouldn't have let me go on a horse without any experience. She is supposed to be looking after me. I want to blame someone. I am going to die young, like Christopher? I don't want to be a ghost, not yet anyway. I think Ed will be cured and grow old and remember me. I mean I don't think my Mum and Dad could lose both their children. Then I think of Stephen and Sarah on the gravestone. But I can't dismount, I'm like a soldier going into battle, who knows he might be killed but he just has to ride on.

Its better when we get to Ashton Court and there's grass and old oaks and its as though we're supposed to be there and being on a horse seems quite natural. As though we live in the big house which is Ashton Court itself and is still there and painted yellow. There's a wedding spilling out with a bride in a satin dress and little white bridesmaids like petals on the lawn. I feel above people who aren't on horses, even wedding guests. We pass another woman on a horse coming the other way and she feels like a friend and says hello though I don't know her. Perhaps the others do. Its as if we only speak to people on horses which I know sounds prejudiced, horsist even, and if I wasn't on a horse I wouldn't be impressed by people who were. A hot air balloon they were only just blowing up when we came in is up in the air and moving away and waving to people on the ground as if they were the queen. Perhaps they're being balloonist. I watch it getting smaller like it was an art lesson about perspective and for a minute I forget I'm on a horse. I know they're higher up than me but it doesn't feel like it. Grandad gets cross with horses on the road he says roads are for cars. Gran says there were roads before cars and horses have to get from field to field. He says, 'Let them use bridleways.'

We do use a bridleway that goes through the wood. I'd never noticed bridleways before. They're like cycle ways but with a picture of a horse instead of a bike which seems obvious now. The posts in the woods have horseshoes painted on them. Its like a special language just for us.

Failand is quite bossy, telling me what to do, till Kate says, 'leave her alone.' Failand says she's promised Jenny, my Gran she means, to look after me and I feel a bit annoyed with Gran but also grateful because I am scared of falling off. I'm quite scared of lots of things, theme parks rides particularly so I'm not surprised. I'm actually more surprised I'm not actually screaming. When I went to Alton Towers with Sophe, I was screaming, not just fun screaming, real fear screaming. Sophe said, 'You may be my best friend Mattie but you're no fun on a ride.'

'You've never ridden before have you?' says Kate a bit shocked as though she's never met anyone so deprived.

'No but I've read Black Beauty,' I say, which is meant to be a joke but I'm not sure if they think it is.

Though I'm feeling nervous I'm also rather pleased with myself and we go past a deer park with the deer looking silver in the sun and I almost think I could be someone who lived in Ashton Court, not a servant as they probably wouldn't ride a horse more a daughter who went out riding before breakfast and met a handsome cousin who says how I the last time he saw me I was a child now I've grown up into a beautiful young woman. I told you I was feeling better.

My horse is called Hailey. 'I hope its not after the comet,' I say.

'Hailey is a complete wimp,' says Kate and I'm glad as that makes two of us. I'm beginning to feel safe, confident almost, when some boys on muddy bikes with helmets come by. They look like they're going to swerve into us on purpose and I don't feel above it all after all. I feel exposed like meeting someone really aggressive on top of a cliff. But they just call out and I think they probably think I'm showing off because I'm on a horse but they're only asking where some woods are. I don't suppose they're as impressed by me being on a horse as I am. When Failand tells them where the woods are I realise its the same one's I went to with Gran that used to be fields. I could have told them myself. Now I really do feel like I live here. Then my mobile goes and I don't want to let go of the reins to answer it but Kate stops, my horse stops too, a bit too suddenly. I hope its Sophe but its Gran saying are you alright and sounding worried. Apparently Grandad came home and said she shouldn't have let me go. I say I'm fine though I'm not sure its true. Actually answering the phone was the nearest I came to falling off. How ironic would that have been?

When we get out of the woods Kate and Failand speed up a bit and it was like when we were on a plane once coming in to land and just when I'd got my confidence up, there was this turbulence and it couldn't land because the airport was full up or something so it kept going round and round. Dad said it was wasting fuel and keeping the air fares up. Ed said it was a wasting the planet.

'That's why it's called a plane it uses up so much of planet,' he said like it was a crossword clue.

Mum said she just wanted to get back down to earth as though we were spacemen. I just wanted to say, slow down like in the car which my father hates me saying. He says he has to go as fast as the rest of the traffic. Sometimes it feels everything's going too fast. Ed says, 'You've got to stay with the herd like a zebra otherwise you get picked off by the lions.'

Now Kate says, 'Slow down Fay, its not fair to Mattie.' I am slowing the herd like a baby elephant bumbling along. I feel happier all the same and I like Kate better now I've gone a mile in her procession. But I was happier still when we got back and I got off, like a soldier coming home from the war, lucky to be alive.

I was hoping we'd go back to Failand's house and Miles would be there but Kate said lets go to hers which was nearer the stables. We had to take the horses back of course and unsaddle them and rub them down and everything, like parking a car. Well more trouble but you know when you go somewhere, on holiday or to a festival how parking seems to take up more time than getting there. Like making sandwiches takes more time than eating them.

'Its like parking a car,' I said but I could see neither of them agreed with me. Hailey already felt like my horse and once I'd got off I could almost understand why girls fell in love with their horses. I wanted to kiss her but I just said, 'Thanks,' like you do to the driver when you get off a bus even though I was aching all over and felt sort of shaky but so relieved.

'You look as though you've been in a serious accident,' Failand's laughing. She sounded more like a friend. Well I had ridden a mile in her company.

Kate's house is a new house and she's got lots of stuff and a sister called Rose who's older and not like Kate. I mean more like Sophe and we talk about clothes. Well me and Rose do. Kate and Failand talk about horses.

'I was going to be a nun till I discovered riding,' says Kate.

'I was going to be a nun till I discovered boys, ' says Rose. They go to a single sex Catholic school apparently and they haven't got any brothers so maybe they don't see a lot of boys. But I don't think it would take them long to catch up.

Rose is taking down some ballet shoes she's got pinned to the wall.

'Your ballet shoes!' says Kate sounding shocked, as though the shoes were symbolic, like she'd had her feet cut off and they were the only reminder of her dancing days.

'I've grown out of pink,' she says. Well she has grown out of the shoes which are very small.

'And you a rose?' says Failand.

'Roses aren't all pink,' said Rose. She's wearing a yellow T shirt. Bright yellow with "I'm a catwalk chick," written on the back. I think it ought to be a catwalk kitten.

'I'm a yellow rose of Texas,' she says in an American accent.

'More dandelion yellow,' says Kate. Then she remembers a donkey called Dandy she went on at Weston when she was about three and knew riding was her thing. They go back to horse talk. Rose talks to me about my T shirt which is one Ed gave me for my birthday and has stars and planets on. I'm not an expert on clothes, which Rose soon realises. She asks me why I'm here and I say about Ed being in hospital and she seems interested but I don't want to talk about him being ill I mean as though that's what he is, an ill person. As though he wasn't like us or a boy she might fancy and want to go out with.

When we go back there's no excuse to go to Failand's house even though I can see Miles in the garden in a hammock looking like someone at home. You know like he's going to be on Stars in Their Eyes or something. This is Miles at home with his sister who likes horses and her friend, that's me, and he's captain of his school cricket team and cut to a picture of him bowling, then back to the hammock and Miles saying his favourite hobby is just hanging around.

Its very hot by now and Gran's got tea on the lawn which is quite thoughtful of her but I really wanted to get out of the sun and I see a fly land on a sandwich.

'Whats this then, in honour of our grand daughter? We don't usually eat al fresco,' says Grandad.

'We don't usually get the weather for it.'

I don't think Gran wants to look as if she's making a fuss. Perhaps she's feeling glad I didn't fall off the horse and break my neck and she'd have to tell my parents like something on the news about someone looking after their grandson who drowned in their gold fish pond. How did they tell his parents that!

Gran says Grandad doesn't appreciate it because he really wants to watch the cricket with his tea. But he says he likes to enjoy the garden for a change.

'It would be more enjoyable if you cut the grass,' says Gran

'At least we've still got some grass, everyone else has gone patio potty and its all car space and decking, this is an original garden.'

'You can say that again, if everything was left up to you there'd only be plain crisps,' says Gran.

'D'you want the last sandwich Matty?' asks Grandad to change the subject. I wonder if its the one the fly was on but I eat it anyway. After all I've survived the horse riding. I'm having a dangerous day.

Gran goes on about how she can remember her Dad cutting the lawn on Sundays and making Christopher do it when you had to push lawnmowers by hand and he'd leave it to go out birds nesting or to collect golf balls and there'd be a row. Then she says her Dad was a bit hard on Christopher and I can see she's nearly crying. I don't know if its for Christopher or her father who must have been sorry when his son died. Then she gets up and goes inside saying she's got a photo somewhere of them all having tea on the lawn, her Mum and Jackie and Christopher.

When she's gone Grandad says, 'Sorry about your Gran she does tend to live in the past.' I think of Christopher who is living in the past or more in the present in the past.

'D'you believe in ghosts?' I ask Grandad.

'No.'

'Did you ever meet Gran's brother who died,' I ask as though I didn't know his name.

'No.'

He says he didn't meet Gran till she was seventeen. Though I can think of Gran being a little girl I can't think of her being seventeen.

'He must have been here in this garden," I go on and look round for him as though I expect to see him which I do. Grandad doesn't of course but he looks worried.

'Less of this ghost talk, don't push your Gran she's never got over it,' he says then but he doesn't say what happened. Then I think maybe she should have got over it because people do die, all of us, and people get over it.

'Where did you meet Gran?' I ask thinking of them in a lover's lane with a gate and a haystack and a moon like someone on leave in a war film. But he says she was a friend of his sister Pat and they'd met at a dance in Bristol.

'Is she dead?' I mean his sister Pat, as I've never met her but I have heard of her.

'No she's living in Canada, we're not all dead,' he says a bit snappily as though I was obsessed with death. Well spotted Grandad! I ask what she was like. Gran I mean, not his sister.

'Not much of a dancer to be honest.' Which doesn't sound very romantic. A little brown butterfly goes past with another butterfly behind it.

'More like a butterfly.' He says.

'Very pretty?' I ask because of the butterfly and old people are always saying how pretty they were when they were young because they don't have to prove it though sometimes you see photos of them and they just look really old fashioned. Except for Elvis. Who looks like Elvis.

'Couldn't keep still,' he says and one of the butterfly's flutters off to a fallen apple, there's two snails on the apple already. Its more popular than the flowers.

'Of course it must have been very hard for your Gran losing her brother like that, I don't think I appreciated it at the time.'

I want to say like what? When he says losing does he mean losing as in dying or losing as in disappearing. Lots of people just go missing or brothers and sisters who get separated when they're babies and get adopted by different parents or go to Australia and find each other on the internet and get reunited for real. Like if Ed went away to get cured in America or somewhere and decided to live there and I didn't see him again till I was sixty one and he was sixty three. Well I don't think that could happen now but it was different then. I mean Gran and Christopher couldn't text each other or email, they just might have lost touch. I know they had telephones and post but I don't think people wrote letters so much then, except old poets who wrote them all the time.

Gran brings out some raspberries and more hot water for the tea. She's got a photo of the garden, one of those little black and white ones so you can't really see what anyone looks like. Just three children and their mother all looking young including the garden and I try to see if Christopher is my ghost but really it could be anyone, though not any time.

'Photography's come on a bit since that was taken,' says Grandad.

'So's the hedge, if my Dad could see it now, and he never had a cordless hedge trimmer.' But she doesn't sound as if she cares really. Grandad picks up the tray and mumbles something about the cricket score.

'Where is your Dad? He's not in the photo.'

'He was taking the picture.' Which makes sense and Ed would have already pointed out. I think of Ed and my Mum and Dad and all the photos we've got and I want to go home to prove they're still there not just on photos. I imagine sneaking off in the night and catching a train. But then everyone would think I'd been abducted or murdered and have to call the police and go on television and make an appeal which wouldn't be very nice for my parents with Ed ill or Gran who's brother disappeared. So I don't.

'The apple tree looks a lot smaller,' I say going back to the photo, feeling like a detective. Surprising myself for noticing.

'Trees tell the time,' she says.

'That philosophy course paid off,' says Grandad.

Marley the cat comes out to join us and catches the butterfly.

'He's eaten that butterfly,' she says sounding shocked. Grandad smiles and I start laughing.

'What's funny about that? She sounds a bit annoyed.

'Grandad said you were like a butterfly.' I explain.

'Oh did he?' But she doesn't sound impressed.

I ring home but only get the answer phone. I think if Christopher's in my room I'll ask him how he got there and if he's dead or what, like he's been messing me about. I want to take it out on someone. It might as well be a ghost who I won't have to answer to, well not in this life. He doesn't appear. I look out of the window and watch Marley who's trying to catch moths. I don't go to sleep for ages and when I do I dream I'm trying to get home but I can't find my house because I'm in the past and the house hasn't been built yet. I wake up feeling lost.

I read a book, not Jandy Mac but one I brought with me, its about a girl of mixed heritage who has a row with her mother and goes to Africa to try to find her real Dad. She can't find him and Africa isn't quite like she expected it to be. Which is like my dream. If she can get to Africa I can get to Yorkshire. But its a book and anyway no one's stopping me going to Yorkshire. I expect Grandad would drive me up there tomorrow if I asked him.

CHAPTER SEVEN

Grandad's gone to work by the time I get up. He comes home at lunch time.

'Mustn't waste the sun,' he drives us to Wells which has a famous cathedral. Its really ancient and you can feel its oldness and sink into it like snow. I send a card to Sophe because it reminds me of her story about the Taj Mahal and it being a sort of grave. This is more a mass grave but spread over a long time. We see a real monk going up some worn out stone steps. Well I suppose he's real not someone dressed up as a monk.

'Looks like a ghost,' says Grandad.

'You said you didn't believe in ghosts,'

'I do in here.'

There is a lot of atmosphere as though the past is heavier than the present weighing it down like a really fat person on the other end of a seesaw.

' I wouldn't like to live here.' I say, shivering as though it really had snowed. You know how snow changes everything. There's effigies of old bishops in the cathedral and knights and their wives, some are inside little open canopies like garden awnings.

'Warmer in than out,' says Grandad. I spose he means its better to be buried in here than outside but I'm not sure anyway its sunny outside. A woman is lighting a candle and praying, murmuring to herself anyway or whoever she's lighting a candle for. She's very tall and slim from the back with jeans and a good jacket and black hair cut sharply into her neck as though its been painted on. She looks like a model or a painting but when she turns round her face is old and bony as though you can see her skull through the skin. I move back.

'D'you want to light a candle for Ed,' asks Gran.

'No,' I say startled. I feel annoyed with Gran as though she's turning Ed into a dead person. Just because her brother died it doesn't mean mine's going to.

'Ed doesn't believe in God he believes in Doctors,' I say not very politely.

"I didn't mean, just to wish him luck with the operation,' she sounds all flustered and older somehow. I feel a bit guilty

'Someone must have to have built all this,' says Grandad looking up at the vaulted ceiling which does look like a miracle.

'It wasn't so long ago everyone went to Church on Sunday,' says Gran, 'think of it, all the churches full up and little processions of people in hats.'

'And the squire on his best horse,' says Grandad.

'Of course a lot of people still do,' she says as if correcting herself.

'They've just changed their hats,' says Grandad and I think of the Muslims going to Mosques, all those men in white robes and little hats kneeling down like you see on television and really believing in Allah. Perhaps Allah is the true God because people believe in him. Perhaps believing is enough. Then I feel disloyal to my God, only he isn't mine unless I believe in him. But God feels more like history to me. I know people still believe in him, not just the Archbishop of Canterbury. The Queen goes to church a lot and so does Tony Blair I think. If there is a God he might understand if I'm not sure on account of being born at the wrong time. And if I'd been born in another country like China or Africa say before they had missionaries I'd never have heard of him till someone came out to save my soul and it wouldn't be easy to believe strangers though some of them did. Though I'm not sure about the Chinese. Believing there's a dead boy in your bedroom doesn't seem so unlikely when people cleverer than me have believed in angels and elephant gods without ever seeing them. I want to say this but remember Joan of Arc got burnt at the stake for hearing voices. Though I think she's a Saint now.

'Its so peaceful here,' says Gran looking out on an old Yew tree with some tidy graves.

'Religion has lot to answer for,' says Grandad. I think of Henry the VIII destroying the monasteries and then about the people blown up on the Tube and a bus in London. But I don't think that's God's fault. Like he's just an excuse. I mean if he did make us and everything it would be like making a tiger and then expecting it not to eat other animals.

We go through the shop and I buy a bookmark with a picture of Jesus in a stream of light as though he's just come in through a stained glass window. The shop leads into the tea room which has gravestones on the wall but the cakes are nice. They sound like important people, the ones on the wall memorials and I don't suppose they knew they'd end up as part of a café. The woman with the skull face is eating chocolate cake.

Its sunny outside and there's a moat with ducks and swans and a big cedar tree and it must look the same to us as it did to the people in the graves. Cedar trees live longer than people.

'The swans used to ring the bell for bread,' says Gran 'They don't now. I suppose it wouldn't be considered dignified, like having to beg.'

'I bet they'd ring it for a bit of fillet steak with a chips and a decent pint,' says Grandad. There was a lot of uneaten bread people had thrown in the water that even the ducks were ignoring though a pigeon with a bad foot was eating it.

'You hardly ever see one who hasn't got walking difficulties,' says Gran and Grandad says shut up because there's a woman in a wheelchair and he think Gran's talking about her, so do I, till she says, 'Still they've got wings,' and I realise she means the pigeons. I hope the woman does.

In the street a man sitting by the wall of the cathedral in a little alcove who asks us for change. Grandad gives him fifty pence.

'You shouldn't he'll spend it on drugs.'

'He couldn't get a cup of tea for fifty pence never mind cocaine, anyway he's traditional,' says Grandad

'I suppose this is where beggars used to sit asking for alms when all the money was spent on building fancy churches,' says Gran and seems to feel happier about the fifty pence as though he was a tourist attraction. He's got a beard and a pipe, an instrument I mean not something to smoke. Now he picks it up and blows it as though we'd put a coin in the slot.

'Now look what you've done.' Gran winces.

We go in a pottery shop where you can tell them your name and they paint it on while you're waiting if it isn't already there.

'I never could find one with Matilda or Edmund on,' said Gran, 'I used to look when you were little. It's a bit late now.'

'I don't expect Failand's Gran even bothered to look.' I said. Which made Grandad laugh. He said they shouldn't have called her Failand.

'Why not there's an India in year seven who isn't an Indian,' I say.

'That's different.' Grandad said.

'Why?' said Gran

He didn't answer for a while then said, 'Failand's too close to home.' He thought this was a very good joke. And we all started laughing till people looked at us. But staying close to home made me feel sad because I wasn't.

'I feel a long way from home.' I say and I find I'm crying though I don't feel sad really.

'Lets all go in the phone box and ring up your Mum together,' says Gran.

Grandad said how the phone boxes were always empty now because everyone had mobiles. Gran said about how she lost hers on a trip to Westonbirt . I ask if Westonbirt is in Weston where we went the last time we came.

'No it's a fancy wood you pay to go into and all the leaves were falling.'

'I expect its ringing still,' said Grandad and then has this idea of ringing it up to see if it answers or if anyone's picked it up and are using it. Of course no one can remember the number. It sounds like a ghost phone buried beneath the leaves, still listening.

There's some gold tiles on the pavement to show where a woman who must have come from Wells jumped in some old Olympic games.

'Long jump,' says Grandad attempting to jump it.

'They only let him out on Wednesdays, and it's a full moon tonight,' says Gran to a woman who's stopped to stare.

'Silly old fool,' the woman says to her friend. I don't know if she means Gran or Grandad?

I feel better squashed into the old red box talking to Mum. When I'm talking to Mum she sounds close as though she's there and you don't have to say anything special just where you are and what you're doing like if you're late coming home from school. When we come out of the phone box she feels a long way away again as though the phone box is a magic box. Now its shut and I wish I'd used it better, like people in stories who get three wishes and waste them. I suppose it would seem magic to some of those people buried in the cathedral.

A woman walks by she's on her mobile saying. 'No I can't. I'm in Wells, I can't be in two places at once can I?' But I think she can, its what phones are for.
Gran says she's got to sit down and there is a seat but woman is sitting on it, an old fashioned looking woman in a lacy white dress like someone in a play. I think it might be Street theatre or something, I saw some young people people looking dressed up earlier but they were more like festival people, like they'd been left over from Glastonbury. This one's wearing gloves and feeding the pigeons.

'Perhaps not, it looks like rain and I don't e want to disturb Miss Havisham" she says.

'Who's Miss Havisham?' I ask thinking its someone Gran knows but doesn't want to talk to.

'Oh just something out of Dickens,' says Gran and of course I think of Sophe saying 'Its what Nans say,' I want to text Sophe and tell her my Gran did actually say something Nans say. I start laughing and Grandad says, 'Whats so funny,? Miss Havisham really is a character in Dickens apparently. A woman who was going to be married and didn't but stayed in her room in her wedding dress with her cake going stale, well I don't think wedding cakes go stale, more like Christmas puddings you can keep them for next year. Anyway I can't get all that into a text, I'm not very good at texting.

It starts to rain really hard so we go back to the car park and there's little streams in the street. Not because of the rain, they were there before only I hadn't noticed them till the rain made them full up. I ask what they're for. Grandad says they were probably for when people wanted to swill things away like when they emptied their chamber pots out of the window.

'Blood from the butchers,' says Gran. We are going past a butchers. I wish she hadn't said that turning meat back into dead animals. But its working for the rain. Perhaps its to stop flooding. We can't find the car when we get to the car park. I think Grandad's getting too old to be out and can't remember where he left it. But we can't find it anywhere. Its been stolen.

'A town of Saints and one of them steals my car,' says Grandad.

'The Saints are dead,' says Gran. The car park attendants aren't very helpful either.

We have to go to the police station to report it and then to the bus station in the really hard rain and wait for a bus. Also it means I can't ask to go home now. I feel cut off. Gran says we were supposed to be going to Weston tomorrow and Grandad is in a bad mood. Actually I quite like it on the bus watching the other people and a girl talling loud on a mobile telling her friend about a dress she's bought to wear tonight and she's worried it wont fit because she didn't try it on. Then she rings up another friend and tells her exactly the same thing then someone she knows gets on the bus and she gets it out to show her. By now the whole bus is interested. Its dark green satin, Gran says it looks like underwear. Its still raining and we're behind a girl on a horse and the horse is having a wee in the rain as it goes along.

'Pissing down,' says Grandad and cheers up a bit at his own joke. A man gets on at a lonely bus stop who Grandad used to go to work with, but he hasn't seen for ages. The man says about someone they both know who's son's been killed in Iraq. They talk about the war in Iraq. And I don't want to think of people dying now, in Iraq, not just in old churchyards long ago. When he gets off we see a fox in a field in the rain. Gran says about how when she was a child out in the woods with her brother they saw a fox and were so impressed. Then they met a man they knew, Mr. Oatway who kept chickens and sold eggs which he brought round on his bike on Saturdays. He had a gun. He said he was looking for a fox who'd been stealing his hens. She told them about the one they'd seen and he asked them to show them where. She'd felt all important and took him to where they saw the fox and there was some fox poo, like spoor, and they followed it and it felt like an adventure.

'Two kids with a man with a gun in the woods, he wouldn't get away with it today,' says Grandad.

And then I have this awful feeling that Christopher was shot in the woods in mistake for a fox, that Gran's just sort of working up to it, she's going to say it, now, on the bus. I don't want her to. But she just says how they saw the fox again and Mr. Oatway shot it and there it was dead. Their beautiful fox. She was so upset and cried for ages and Christopher said she'd betrayed the fox and it reminded her of the war in Iraq.

'How?' asked Grandad.

'We don't think things through,' said Gran. She said she still regretted saying about the fox all these years later though it seemed a good idea at the time.

'What about the people killed on the London Underground?' says Grandad.

'And what about Mr. Oatway's hens.' I didn't know if they were supposed to represent the people blown up in London.

'And now there's Ray's son,' she added and you could see there'd always be a reason for war.

'I remember when Ray's boy was born. He came into work so chuffed, 'Bristol City here we come,' he said, he wanted a boy.

'What's wrong with girls?' asked Gran.

'Nothing, but he already had three,' says Grandad.

I hoped he still had the three girls, well they would be women by now. There'd be grandchildren probably. Then the bus gets held up by an accident. We all look out of the window as we go past. A car's gone into a horsebox.

'I knew there'd be a horse involved,' says Grandad, he sounds quite triumphant.

When we get back it's still raining. There's a programme on television about people throwing all their old stuff away, de-cluttering they call it.

'You could get rid of some of the stuff in Mattie's room,' says Grandad. I feel really worried. What if she throws out Christopher's toys. But Gran says she isn't throwing anything away they can put it on her funeral pyre if they like.

'Of course you don't want to throw out the baby with the bathwater,' says Grandad. Which I didn't get but its definitely one for what Nan's say. I start thinking of Christopher like a doll in a children's book who comes out and has adventures then gets back into the toy box when the children come home. Its as if Christopher could be thrown out too. What about the Pied Piper leading all the children away, which doesn't seem so bad as they're all together and at least they think they're going somewhere nice. Some days I wish I believed in heaven. Some days I do, but not today. When Jesus died they had a big stone that was rolled away when he rose from the dead. I think of the stones in the cathedral, if one of those stone figures got up in the night? But it would only be like a horror film or vandalism.

I get upstairs and find Christopher in the bedroom. He's made a paper plane which he calls an aeroplane.

'This is my room if you don't mind and could you clear up some of your stuff.' I say sounding mean though actually I'm quite relieved to see him.

'Sorry but I'm not taking up any room,' Which sounds sad, or is he being sarcastic. I feel guilty and think ghosts don't take up any room but they do take it over if they haunt it. Which I want to say but I haven't got anyone to say it to except a ghost. Which would sound rude. I could say it to Ed if he wasn't ill, the trouble with Ed being ill is you have to be careful what you say.

'Well no one lives forever,' I say as I think Christopher's playing the ghost card. But then I'm not even sure if he knows he's a ghost, I could ask him how he died. No I cant. There's some things only the person who's involved can say.

I think of Abe in our class who behaves like he's the only black boy in the world though he's not even the only one in our class.

Sophe said, 'He wasn't even the blackest,' He used to be before Samson came from Kenya. Being in our class is like when Snow White's stepmother asks, 'Who's the fairest?' It keeps changing. Christopher is the only ghost I've ever met. I wonder how Sophe would cope with Christopher.

'There's nothing wrong with being black,' said Mia who really is the fairest. Though no one said there was, well not me. And all the black children I know are proud of being black.

Mia talks about black people as though they have a terrible time which isn't true, well not in our school. I know they did in history but its now, like you wouldn't get hung for stealing a sheep anymore even if you weren't hungry or even sent to Australia. Mia is a natural blonde but it looks dyed because its so blonde. She sits under a window and the sun shines through it like Rumpleskiltskin has been in and turned straw into gold. I wonder if she sits there on purpose. I never thought of that before.

I only see Christopher in the evening or night time and I wonder if he can't come out in the day like Dracula or if the sunlight would shine through him like Mia's hair.

Abe doesn't need Mia to stick up for him as he's quite capable of doing that himself and he's the one who goes on about being black not us. But I don't say that. He's popular with the boys because he's good at football and popular with the girls because he's gorgeous. He has this sexy smile which might be stereotyping but so did Elvis Presley. Abe and Sophe are always arguing but they seem to enjoy it. When we had a lesson abut slavery he went on about it as though our great, great, great Grandparents all owned sugar plantations.

Sophe said her great, great, great grandfather had been sent up rich people's chimneys to clean them when he was a boy even though they couldn't afford any coal themselves and all his children had died of hypothermia. Then he'd died in the Charge of the Light Brigade because someone had blundered and you can't blame people for what their ancestors did who've been dead for ages. It'd be like blaming the Queen for Henry the VIII having his wives heads cut off. I don't think you could, not even if you were a direct descendant of Anne Boleyn.

'Is that true?' I asked Sophe, about her great, great, great Grandather not Henry VIII as I do believe that's true even though its quite amazing that anyone married him after Anne Boleyn

'I don't know, he might have, anyway Abe's ancestor might have been a chief who had slaves himself but don't say that because he's bigheaded enough.'

I told Ed, who said it was silly of Sophe to make things up and if all her great great grandfather's children had died of hypothermia Sophe wouldn't be here either which wouldn't be a great loss. I said she can say it, it's a free country. Then he said, 'Anyway its unfashionable.'

I said, 'Who cares about fashion?'

'Sophe,' said Ed as though we were talking about clothes.

I think how different things would be in Christopher's class. How they'd all come from the same village and not have any computers. Just books.

'What' d'you want to be when you grow up?' I say forgetting that he isn't going to grow up.

'A pilot,' he says, 'or an engineer, or an archaeologist,' which is quite ambitious for a ghost. I start crying and I don't know if it's for Christopher who's never going to go in a plane, or Ed being ill. Everyone at home seems far away like I can't ever go back and explain things. As though I wont see Sophe again, only bump into her in years to come in a supermarket or somewhere and we'll say hello and not even go for a coffee. I might be with my husband who'll say, 'Who's that?'

'Oh just someone I went to school with, d'you want the walnut yoghurt there's ten per cent free.'

CHAPTER EIGHT

Next day Failand rings and says they're having a barbecue that evening if I want to come. I do want to go especially as I think Miles will be there. So I say yes please. Then I'm trying to think of something to wear. I look in the wardrobe where I've put all my clothes and start trying tops on, but I get a bored. I notice the cupboard where Gran said the dinky toys may have come from. I've never opened the cupboard. I found the books in the wardrobe. I get the feeling that Christopher might be in there. Locked in there. He might live in there like Anne Frank in her secret room. I think of skeletons in closets. What if I opened the cupboard and he fell out, sort of dead but preserved somehow, not purposely like an Egyptian, but by accident like that person they dug out of a bog, which Ed went on about when it was on television. I ring Ed which I've been wanting to but not to just say about his treatment. I think the bog man is a good excuse. As if I was doing a project. I ask him why he should have been preserved when lots of people who've died since haven't.

'Being in the right place at the right time, the optimum conditions I suppose,' he says. I'm not quite sure what he means by optimum conditions but its nice to talk to him about something that isn't about being ill.

'But why only him? ' I feel I'm getting somewhere.

'Perhaps its like winning the lottery, someone's got to do it.'

Which is a change as he usually says about how many people have to lose. But it does make sense as if everyone who died, died in a bog and their body was preserved there'd hardly be room for babies. Then we talk about other things. I say about the horse and he thinks me riding a horse is funny and says how I was scared on a donkey in Scarborough when I was little and screamed so much the donkey man had to stop the donkey for me to get off in the middle of a ride. That must have been a first. I feel happy when he laughs and then he says he's made friends with a boy in hospital, Leo, who's really funny and cool though he probably won't get better. Leo that is. And I say about Christopher, not about him here being a ghost but about him being Gran's dead brother and his old dinky toys are still here in the cupboard.

'That's a bit grim for you.'

I don't say it's not as grim as having a dying boy for a friend. Then he says he's got to go he's playing a computer game with Leo. I say I'm going to a barbecue.

 I don't know whether to wear the top Gran bought me or my best dress which is grey linen. It looked good in the shop but it gets very creased and needs a lot of ironing so I've hardly ever worn it. When I did wear it to Luce's fifteenth, Sophe said it made me look like an orphan. I said I had to wear it because it cost so much. She said, when your rich mother comes to find you in the orphanage she'll recognise you because you'll still be wearing the same dress. I miss Sophe.

 Then my mobile goes and it is Sophe. I'm telepathic! She's going to a barbecue tonight herself with Luce and a boy called Connor who is Luce's boyfriend and drives a car. She's wearing a lemon top, 'really sharp.' she says, and I think of lemons being sour so my mouth contracts, and I am impressed by the powers of suggestion. I try to tell Sophe but she's going on about a denim skirt, really short. I say about my barbecue and should I wear the grey dress. She says, its one thing to say what Nan's say but not to wear what Nan's wear. I decide to wear it anyway. It's a dress. I mean jeans are too easy. Gran says I look very nice which Sophe would say only proved her point. But I look in

68

the mirror and think I do look nice in a quiet sort of way. A girl on a book cover who's clever but wants to be pretty. I'm not very clever but I think I'm pretty enough. I mean I don't work on it and nobody's perfect.

Then Gran says, 'What shall I wear?' which surprises me, as I hadn't thought she'd be coming. Then we take more time deciding what she'll wear than I did. She tries on an orangey skirt with a frill but she says it makes her look like a mermaid.

'More like a salmon,' says Grandad.

In the end she wears dark green linen trousers and a lighter green top, sort of posh T shirt with satiny stripes in it which looks quite good, well for a pensioner. Actually Gran looks quite young, for her age I mean and considering she's fat, well not fat club fat or anything but not slim like Sophe's Nan. Her Nan does wear jeans and goes on about what to put on till Sophe says, 'You're going to bingo not the ball.'

Grandad wears a dark red shirt the colour of wine. He takes some wine. Gran says she read somewhere that people don't take wine to parties anymore. Grandad says he'll take a chance, he'd sooner look out of date than tight. Its Nina's fortieth birthday apparently so its not a children's party. Its only next door and there's quite a few older people sat on a wooden gallery round one of those patio heaters like big mushrooms they have in Pub gardens. There's an awning with strings of lanterns and ropes of light and candles floating in the pond. It looks really pretty and hard to believe it's the next door garden like its hard to believe it's the next door house. Nina comes to meet us in a red and white spotted dress.

'Very 1950's.' says Gran. I do worry about Gran but Nina doesn't seem to mind.

'More Marilyn Monroe than Doris Day, I hope?' she says.

I was thinking Minnie Mouse, but I didn't say anything.

'She looks she's just come back from the farm shop, and about to bring round the organic apple pie,' Failand says to me but it's Maria who comes round with a tray of little savoury tarts, which Gran say taste homemade.

'But not in this home,' says Failand. She's wearing a thin filmy dress, very pale pink, the skirt is shaped like petals, like a flower fairy if you ever read the flower fairy books, which I did, once upon a time. Gran's sister, Auntie Jackie gave me a boxed set. I've kept them because I like the pictures and they do tell you all about flowers. Failand's hair is tucked up like a ballet dancers. I'm surprised she's dressed up. She looks like someone else or like herself grown up and married to someone rich.

'More Fey than Failand,' says Gran, Gran's going to get us sent home.

Kate's wearing a white cotton top with tucks and things like a Victorian nightdress or a doll on Antiques Road Show that someone's old Auntie left them once and now they're an old Auntie themselves. She's wearing it over white shorts so it looks like she hasn't put her skirt on yet. Rose is wearing a short sticky out skirt with a silvery satin top with a sequinned star like she might do a dance on X factor and she's curled her hair in droopy hanging down curls and looks really pretty but quite old. She is fourteen. My dress is beginning to look like I've come straight from school and I want to be librarian when I grow up.

Miles is there with his guitar and a black boy called John who's got one of those heads that some black boys have, like a sculpture, which I find myself staring at because I like art. I think Gran could paint him.

'Haven't you seen a black person before? Welcome to the darkside.' He sounds annoyed. I want to tell him it was about his head not his skin colour but I don't think I'll get away with it. I do stare at people. One day I was on a bus staring at this woman because she was so old, and really wrinkled and she had her hair in a bun and I thought how she was like an old woman in a fairy story who gives the nasty brother good advice but he wont take it from an old woman but the good brother does and gets to marry the princess. Then she says, the old woman on the bus I mean, not the fairy story one.

'Had your penny's worth or d'you want you money back?' I'm not sure what she meant but I was sure she was annoyed. Sophe thought it was very funny and kept saying it.

I wish she was here or anyone else from my school. I used to go round with Chloe a lot who's mixed race but not very mixed. I never thought of her as a black girl. She isn't. Her skin is white. Her mother is white and so is her brother. Well he's got red hair. Once when a man with a Scottish accent was in their house rowing with her mother and I said, 'Is that your Dad?' she laughed and said it wasn't her Dad, it was her brother's Dad, her Dad was West Indian. I hadn't noticed. Well not till then. When I said about it, about me not noticing, she said, 'So what, its no big deal,' which I didn't think it was but I did think it was interesting. Like Grandad going on his ancestry site to find out about who his his ancestors were. Somehow we were never quite friends after that. So I must have said something wrong somehow.

I go to a multiracial school and it's more Muslims at our school especially in year one and two. I know its a religion not a race but it is mostly children from Pakistan. We don't mix all that much, the Asians and the Europeans I mean. Its like boys and girls, they don't mix all that much but it doesn't mean they think they're better than each other. Well actually they both think they're better than each other so it cancels out. Sometimes its because English isn't their first language. I can't explain all that obviously. I just want to say it isn't that easy being white because they can go on about being different but we cant. John lives in Clifton, which is a posh part of Bristol and goes to the same school as Miles and speaks like him. Miles and John are both wearing black T shirts and black jeans which makes John look like a shadow. I want to say this, but only to Sophe, though she might say I'm making a thing about it.

Perhaps he's only joking about the dark side, trying to be scary? He's setting up his drum kit and Rose is sat by him on a little stool gazing at him in dreamy way so it looks like they're in film set in New York. Miles and John are in the band and waiting for another boy called Josh who isn't here yet.

They start talking about names for the band. They're called Tomboys but they want to change it because the boy called Tom who started the band has left.

'You should call it something local,' says Gran. And I feel embarrassed by her joining in. Which probably makes me ageist as well.

'Like Portishead, like its been done.' says Miles.

'Clevedon Pier or Weston Super Mare.' says Gran and I think what Sophe would think about calling a band something your Nan says.

'Weston Super Stallions,' says Rose looking at John again. With more stars in her eyes than on her top.

'Clevedon Pier, playing tonight, that'll bring the crowds back,' now Grandad's joined in, he's coming by with a pint and happy camper smile. Actually I think it sounds alright.

'You could call it Failand Road,' says Failand.

'One Failand in this house is enough.' says Miles.

'What d'you want, English Rose?' John asks Rose in an edgy kind of way.

'Irish Rose, I was called after my grandmother, she was from County Cork,' says Rose in an Irish accent.

'Not Grandma roses?' says Kate who is her sister so she's allowed.

'How about, Katherine the Great?'

'What egos,' says John. 'The Long Ashton Airheads,' and I don't know if he's suggesting it for name or calling them it, which is what a name is I suppose.

'Clifton Village,' says Rose helpfully which is where John lives. He sighs and I think he might want something from his country of origin wherever that is. Don't worry I'm not going to ask.

'You could have a contradiction like, like… Hard Feathers,' says Kate which I think is quite clever.

'Soft Bricks,' says Miles and they all laugh at this amazing joke which I don't see.

'Say it fast,' says Failand. I do, out loud and they all laugh again because it sounds like soft pricks and I feel embarrassed. For not seeing it I mean not for saying it. I have said worse things than that

Then Josh arrives and he says, 'Nempnett Thrubwell' which everyone thinks is a good name and is a place near here which I haven't heard of but they have.

'Who comes from Nempnett Thrubwell?' I ask.

'No one, that's the point,' says Kate, though I couldn't see what the point was.

'What's it famous for? I know Cheddar's famous for cheese,' I nearly say they could call it Hard Cheese but I manage to stop myself. I've said too much already

'Its famous for being called Nempnett Thrubwell that's why Josh suggested it, duh,' says Failand as though she's lost patience with me. I feel upset. I wish Sophe was here or

I wasn't. I'm glad Ed isn't, he'd say I'd really ballsed it up. I drink some wine which is on the table and I don't care what any one thinks anymore.

'My Grandad came from there that's why I said it,' says Josh. He says it to me and he says like he can't understand what they're on about either. Josh talks like you might expect a farmer's boy to talk. Well a west country one, like he's just going to milk the cows or muck out the pigs. I think he might not go to the same school as Miles and John. He's got short black hair that sticks up like the Chinese baby's in our Chinese fish and chip shop. He's wearing a black T shirt but his jeans are blue and he's got a lot of spots which doesn't help though obviously people from posh school have spots too and he'll grow out of them but I won't know him then.

'How's your granddad?' Gran asks Josh. She probably went to school with his Grandad who's just had a bypass operation apparently which sounds like another road and I want to laugh. I've finished the whole glass of wine and no ones said anything. I feel quite happy now.

'Any suggestions Mattie?' asks Miles as though he's trying to include me but also as though he's feeling sorry for me.

'Something more anarchic pleeese,' says John

'Blackheads,' I don't know why I say that. Whether it's because of John's head or Josh's spots. I just wish I hadn't. Will they think I'm being racist, or faceist. I mean face-ist not fascist. I don't even know what fascist means but I know its not good. Actually I am being faceist because I definitely don't like Josh's spots and I wouldn't want to kiss him. I don't think either of them want to kiss me. I want to say I'm being anarchic which is another word I'm not totally clued up on. Abe tried to start a gang once called the Blackhand Gang, it never happened. When I told Dad he laughed and when I

74

asked him what was funny he said it was ironic. I don't think Abe meant it to be ironic. No one thinks I'm being ironic. There is an uneasy silence as they say in books. Why did I say it? I think it's the wine. It makes me feel I can say anything I like. But I don't like what I'm saying.

John says, 'Oops she's from up North,' as though coming from Yorkshire was a stigma. I don't know if he's making fun of my accent or saying we're all thick up North which isn't fair. But life isn't fair or Ed wouldn't have leukaemia. He'd be here saying the right thing and fitting in and maybe Rose would fancy him. I feel tears in my eyes and can't say anything. I drink some more wine, I don't know who's, which is on a little table in the porch. Then I knock over a whole bottle.

'Steady girl, steady,' says a man going by, like I'm a horse. I leave the bottle spinning and spilling. I feel the wrong size like Alice in Wonderland. I go to the bathroom but the door's shut and I can hear Hamish talking to himself and pulling the flush and then I see there's water coming out from under the door.

'Let me in Hamish?' I say as I'm feeling sick.

'Go away, go away,' so he can talk. I can see Hamish only talks when he wants to. He doesn't talk for other people as he wouldn't care what they think. I wish I was autistic then I wouldn't care what people thought but I know I shouldn't think that because I wouldn't want to be autistic all the time it would be like wanting to be blind when you saw something horrible. Once I saw a dead man in the road, he'd been killed in a car accident and I kept thinking about him. I wished I hadn't looked but I wouldn't want to be blind just not to have seen him.

I try the door which isn't locked and Hamish is there with his trousers down stuffing whole toilet rolls down the lavatory and pulling the flush on them.

'Get me more toilet paper,' he says in a bossy way but I think he'd say that even if I was the Queen. I don't know what to do. Whatever I do I'll probably get the blame for flooding the house or for telling on Hamish. I mean I don't know what's allowed for him or for me. I do know they probably don't want their toilet blocked.

Then Rose appears and takes over. 'Oh Hamish what are you up to?' but as though its quite normal to be flooding the house with sewage when they've got such a nice house and they're having a party. And there's Rose in her 'dying swan' ballerina skirt as Grandad called it earlier and shoes with glass beads on trying to mop up the toilet like Cinderella getting home early. I should help but I just sort of leave and go back to Gran's house because I feel even sicker and I want to ring up Mum and ask to go back home because I hate it here.

There's no answer from the house and Mum's mobiles switched off. I could try Dad then I think they're at the hospital. Either way I can't ring up and say I want to come home because they'll ask why. I am sick, very sick, in Gran's toilet luckily. Then I go into my bedroom to take my dress off which smells of sick. I put on some jeans and the top Gran bought me but I still don't want to go back. Why hasn't Gran or Grandad come to find me. Nobody cares. I start crying.

'Whats the matter?' Its Christopher appearing like a good fairy. I try to tell him but I don't think he'll understand. Not about saying Blackheads because I'm not sure what is wrong with it and because I don't think he'd understand. He might even think people from Africa are cannibals and eat explorers like in pictures in old comics, like America's still full of cowboys.

'Would you eat someone if you were starving?' There was this film I saw once about a plane crash in the snow where the survivors start eating each other.

'Like on a desert island, probably if they were dead and someone else had cooked them, just slices, and you couldn't see the body?' Christopher says as though he'd thought about it before and I can almost feel I am on a desert island. I wish I was.

'If they weren't related and it was just meat wrapped up in a vine leaf,' he adds like it was a Chef programme.

'Would you eat a cat?' he says as Marley comes in.

' I might but not one I knew.'

'Or if you had to kill it.'

'I wouldn't eat a pig if I had to kill it.' I say and Marley goes out with her tail up and we both laugh. Gran comes in and calls out.

'Are you alright? Why did you come back?'

'I spilt something on my dress, wine I think,'

'I hope you weren't drinking it, I'll have your mother on to me.' But she sounds a bit drunk herself. She says there's been a fuss because Hamish has blocked the lavatory and Toby, his Dad is having to rod the drains or something drastic. Apparently he always does that and usually they don't put much paper out but because it was a party .....

'Sorry I've got to go,' I say to Christopher as I don't want to offend anyone else. But there's no one there.

Its funny how real he seems, like a friend no one's going to approve of who jumps back over the garden wall when the adults appear, like when the servants children didn't play with the children from the big house. Or when they did their parents didn't approve. Neither parents.

I come downstairs and Gran can see I've been crying.

'Whats the matter?' And I start crying again.

'They're ganging up on me because I come from Yorkshire and don't talk posh or go to a posh school,' I say, which I'm not sure is true.

'I feel excluded,' I add which I don't really and I don't like it when children at school say it. Children who don't get picked for something they want to do because they're not very good at it or it isn't their turn. I keep saying things I wish I hadn't. I think it's the wine. So does Gran, she makes me a cup of coffee. She says they aren't that bad or that posh and Miles and John go to Bristol Grammar school and so does Failand though it used to be a boys only school when she was young.

'They've got everything,' I say. But she says, 'No they haven't and how Toby isn't their father. He's only Hamish's father, their father went to France on some job and met a French girl and never came back but that was before they came to live next door so she's never met him. I'm trying to take this in when Gran says her brother passed the 11-plus and got a place at Bristol Grammar school but he never got to go though they'd bought the uniform. I realise she means Christopher so he must have been eleven when he died, in the summer holidays like now only about fifty years ago. It makes calling the band Blackheads not seem very terrible so I tell Gran who does look a bit shocked but shrugs.

'Well no one will be able to speak to anyone soon,' she says and I said Ed said you had to keep up to date as language was always changing it was like evolution and you'd be left behind, stranded in the past like the last woolly mammoth.

'Ed's too clever for his own good,' she says and looks sad and I wonder if she knows something about Ed I don't. Or is she thinking about Christopher passing the exam to go to grammar school and never getting to go there and I even wonder that happened to the uniform. Did he die doing something clever like an experiment that went wrong.

'There's bound to be teething troubles if you come from somewhere different, you always have to ease yourself in a bit with the natives,' she says then and I realise she means me not John. Like I'm the odd one out and this is a trick question. Like one they might have asked at an old eleven-plus exam. 'Who's the odd one out?' I suppose most people would say Hamish but it could be Josh for wearing blue jeans or John for being of African origin but it's me for not living here.

'But I had noticed John was black,' I say like a confession.

'Of course you did, its not a crime, we all notice if people look different or just buy a new coat otherwise we wouldn't be able to recognise anyone, its just not making such a fuss about it.'

'Well they make more fuss about skin colour than, than, fur colour,' I say as Marley's sat there licking his ginger fur and I think of our cat Spider who's black and white.

' I can't understand why everyone does, but they do, so there must be a reason,' she says which kind of makes sense. I think how many Muslin girls in our school wear scarves but I don't notice, well not anymore.

'I suppose only a cloned sheep wouldn't be recognisable to another sheep,' says Gran and I feel better. We can hear them clapping next door.

'We ought to go back and face the music,' she says ambiguously, 'You're not getting much young company.'

'I haven't walked a mile their procession,' I agree.

'With some people half a mile is more than enough,' and she goes to change her shoes as if she really is going to try and walk a mile with somebody.

CHAPTER NINE

We go back and no one says anything. I mean like they really don't say anything. I wish they would instead of ignoring me. I know they might not be ignoring me on purpose. They probably weren't thinking about me at all and hadn't noticed I'd gone because if you go you usually get forgotten. OK I'm feeling left out again. I want to go back home. Gran and Grandad's house I mean which isn't really home. I'm sat on my own. I'm glad Sophe can't see me

'You've changed, I liked the frock, it had something,' says Rose coming to sit by me. She sounds all friendly and I want to say how pretty she looks but I can't. Even the wine won't say it for me. Perhaps its worn off, the effect of the wine I mean. Or perhaps it was the grey dress, that it did have something, something magic that transported me to another time and I was behaving like a girl in a boarding school in Gran's old children's books. I don't mean they got drunk but they were prejudiced about poor people and patronising to their servants and they may have had a golliwog in their toy box.

'You missed Fay singing, ' Kate makes me feel rude and self centred. Of course she would be able to sing. I think of when you have to write what your hobbies are and I can't think of anything except reading. I expect Failand could fill the page.

'The band is finishing.' Miles says, 'Nempnet Thrubwell have been playing for you for free tonight. Next time you'll have to pay.' They all clap and laugh and everyone seems to know everyone. I clap too and wish I hadn't missed so much.

'Nempnet Thrubwell goes global,' says John, 'I don't think so.' I don't think he likes the name.

'I used to like the Sally Army,' says an old man Grandad's talking to.

'The Tally band, that'd be a good one,' says Grandad. I don't think the boys approve, though I think its quite anarchic. Grandad sounds quite pleased with himself. I wonder if he's drunk.

'Its just a name,' says Miles which coming from their family is a bit much.

'Its on the map,' says Josh and I don't know if he means, 'they're on the map' like they've arrived or just that Nempnet Thrubwell is a place on the map. I don't feel like I'm on the same map. I'd like to ring Sophe but I'll only sound pathetic. I find it hard to believe she's my best friend she feels part of the past like God in the cathedral. Like if you leave your seat and someone else comes and sits in it and it's their seat. Perhaps this is my seat now and these people are my friends or enemies or whatever. As if I was on the wrong bus and I'd have to go where it was going and the only people I'd ever see from now on were these passengers. We'd have to get to know each other. I think this would make a good film. And I wonder who to put in it. I might even put Mia by the window and have a shot of her hair with the sun shining through. But she wouldn't be the star.

Then this woman called Samantha comes up who remembers my father when he was a teenager and she says how she fancied him. Perhaps I've got roots after all, real roots like when Mum buys something in the garden centre in a pot and takes it out to plant and says, 'Good roots.' Maybe once you've got good roots its alright to be transplanted like you can grow anywhere though Mum usually only puts them in a bigger pot. I want to tell someone my roots theory. Ed would understand but he's not here. Then I think of something even worse, that I could live without Ed. Just remember him. 'My brother said that,' I'd say to someone one day. And they'd say, 'I didn't know you had a brother.' And I'd say, 'He died when he was young,' and when they looked shocked I'd say. 'It was a long time ago.' And they'd think I'd forgotten but I wouldn't have. By then my parents would have died and I'd be as old as Gran only I wouldn't look as old as her as everyone would have cosmetic surgery and drugs or operations that kept you young. What if I had a grand daughter who could talk to Ed like I talk to Christopher. Then I feel guilty as if I was trying to turn Ed into a ghost. But I do think we will probably not get old as quick as people do now.

Then this really ancient old man catches hold of my arm.

'I knew your grandmother. A remarkable woman, such a loss, she died without finding him.' As though he was talking about Gran in the past tense as if he could read my thoughts or was another ghost, maybe the ghost of summers yet to come. I don't want anymore ghosts. Christopher is OK he's my ghost. This man isn't a ghost because Grandad's bringing him a drink. I feel sick again and annoyed with the man even if he does have Alzheimars for making me think about Gran being dead.

'She isn't dead she's over there.' I say sharply. He looks confused, then laughs and says, 'Your great grandmother I meant, Elsie, Jenny's mother. I used to live here, in this house, it was different then.' I look confused.

'Mind the generation gap,' says Gran and I do think it might be something you could fall through. I sort of work out that he was my Gran's next door neighbour when my Gran was a girl and he knew her mother and he's probably as old as Mrs. Woolley. Which means he must have known Christopher and how he died but he doesn't seem the best person to ask. He's still mumbling, 'Different then, different then, don't expect I can still find the toilet now.' He gets up, with difficulty and shuffles off and I wonder if the toilet's alright now as I don't think he could cope with Hamish. Then I think he was once a young soldier marching to war with the names on the war memorials.

'Old Charlie, he's Toby's father, he used to live here,' says Gran which means he's Hamish's great grandfather but not Failands' or Miles's. Well I think that's it. I'm having trouble working it out. I feel funny and musty somehow as if there's too much past, like in Wells cathedral.

Josh comes up and says, 'Lighten up we're not that bad,' I don't know if he means their playing or my running away. He's got a foxy face which would be quite nice if he didn't have zits. I can think of him grown up and still living here and married to a local girl and l having lots of children and auctioning cows in a very fast voice like on farming programmes. Like they're still be cows.

'You OK.' He says again as if he'd seen me being sick. I start talking about Ed. I don't know why. I just want to talk to someone, someone my age who's interested. He says there was a boy at his school and everyone thought he was going to die but he was fine now and back in the football team.

'Did he have leukaemia?' I asked.

'No meningitis.' Which wasn't the same but it was in a way. That thinking someone might die doesn't mean they will.

'Come on you two break it up, this is a multi generation party,' said Miles as though we were kissing or something but he sounded friendly and I was glad he'd noticed us. Well me. Actually the old ones are behaving worse than us, laughing and sounding drunk and even dancing. Gran and Grandad seem to know everyone and Samantha who once fancied my Dad is under the veranda with a man. I wonder if she ever……. with my Dad I mean. They would have been teenagers so they might have.

Rose and John are holding hands by a rose arch looking like one of those black and white photos of people kissing in Paris by the Eiful tower Luce had on a birthday card.

Worth a picture anyway, when cameras were more cumbersome. I don't like to take one. Miles does with his mobile.

'I shall be circulating this at school, it may even go global,' and they laugh in an unembarrassed way. Failand is talking about horses to Kate. I can't think of anything to say about horses. I wish I could. I wouldn't normally care but I do now. Some things matter and even if afterwards they turn out not to matter you can't know beforehand even if you have a sixth sense. You'd probably need a seventh sense for that.

I drift over towards Gran and Grandad who's talking to old Charlie. I think of him as old Charlie as though that was his name or there was a little Charlie here. They're talking about the war. Grandad was a war baby so he could only have shaken his rattle. I nearly say so but they look serious and I'm glad I don't. Old Charlie's saying about his friend who was killed so long ago, how he saw him blown up, such a good looking boy and how it's not fair, as though its just happened. I think of James Winter on the war memorial. He could be sitting here now talking about the war or his heart bypass and not being able to find the toilet and it doesn't seem so bad, being dead. I wonder if there's anyone alive who remembers him.

Gran and her friends are talking about the garden. Old Charlie says how he used to grow runner beans and potatoes down there by where the roses are now and how he kept hens where the big blue flowers are. Everybody kept hens then. The women say about the food, how it used to be sausage rolls and prawn vol au vents and a quiche you made yourself at parties. Now its fragrant Thai chicken and sushi bought in Sainsburys. Its all old talk. No one talks to me. Perhaps I'm invisible.

People say they want to be invisible like it would be their first wish but I think they'd sooner be noticed, unless you were on a secret mission or an animal stalking its prey.

'It's the wine talking.' I hear a woman say and I think she means me though I haven't said anything lately, or fallen over. But she's talking to Nina and the parent generation who are talking about holidays and getting cheap flights on the internet and how convenient having the airport so near. Someone says about a restaurant in Barbados built on the beach and seeing turtles while they eat. Grandad tries to butt in by asking about the cricket score in Barbados but he's ignored. People seem to be separated into age groups. I look for mine. They're all engrossed with one another. I'm glad when people start to leave. I pick up a glass of champagne which has been poured out and left from when we all toasted Nina's fortieth birthday. Gran and Grandad bought her bamboo in a yellow pot which Gran said looked Chinese, but I think red is their favourite colour, Chinese people I mean. Its on the balcony now, the yellow pot, and there's a wineglass in it and a bit of sushi which is kind of oriental. I go to look at the gold fish and I think how pretty it is with moths flying about the lights round the pond. How like scenery as though a play was going to start.

Then Miles comes up and says, 'Midsummer's Night's Dream.' and I don't know if he's answering my question or thinking the same as me and everyone's brains are linked like the fishes moving together as though they've been rehearsing for ages.

I say about the fish to Miles who says, 'I think they give off signals or something, on the same wavelength anyway,' and he laughs. He sounds a bit like Ed, like knowing things, but more cool about it. And I feel guilty because I think Ed thinks he's really laid back and wouldn't like me thinking Miles was just as bright but not as heavy. But Ed doesn't know what I'm thinking or that I'm here by the pond in the moonlight. So perhaps we're not that much like the fish.

'I don't suppose fish could have secrets,' I say to Miles who I think is impressed by this as he laughs again as though I'm being particularly witty or he's drunk. I've seen him drinking from a bottle of lager. Then he does something surprising. He kisses me very lightly like a moth and I feel a reaction like the fish giving off signals and I want him to kiss me again but less like a moth. He doesn't.

'Come on your Gran's going to think I'm taking advantage,' he pulls me by the hand. I want him to take advantage. Then I see Grandad who seems to be lurching a bit leaning over the balcony like he's on a ship in a storm. A drunken sailor?

'Come on young 'un we can't have you leading the locals astray.' I'm glad he sort of blames me not Miles as it would have been embarrassing. Not that we were doing anything but I feel happier all over and just laugh and say, Goodnight, to Miles and even remember to say, 'Thanks for the party,' to Nina who I pass on the steps. At this point I trip over but it doesn't seem to matter. It looks like anyone could trip over and Toby, who's now old Charlie's grandson as well as Hamish's dad, pulls me up.

'Now you're not going to sue are you?' as though it was the step's fault.

I look back at the lights on the trees.

'Your garden looks like Christmas in summer.' I say and I can almost hear Sohpe groan. Toby has turned back to Hamish who's pouring wine over the balcony so I don't think he heard me.

CHAPTER TEN

I sleep late and when I wake up I get a weird feeling that I live here. That I've lived here always I mean, like Gran. That my real home doesn't exist. Then Gran says Mum has rung to say Ed is having his operation today. Well its not an operation exactly more a tube replacing his blood and bone marrow. I've seen the video. I feel guilty because I've forgotten its today. It was on the calendar in red at home. Gran looks worried. Then Christopher appears downstairs. He's sat in a chair looking at a comic called the Eagle. He looks so real I think Gran and Grandad must be able to see him but obviously they can't or one of them would mention it.

'Have you met our resident ghost?' they'd say, a bit embarrassed.

I'd have to pretend I met ghosts every day like you do when you meet someone strange and pretend they aren't. When Luke, my cousin was in an accident, we went to see him. He was covered in spokes like a walking bicycle but we acted as if it was normal. Well till we were going home and me and Ed started laughing and we couldn't stop. He's Ok now, Luke, they've taken the spokes out but he isn't in the football team anymore.

I want to say about Christopher myself. I don't because they might think I'm making it up, 'I can see your dead brother in that chair.' Like I was making fun of him, I mean Christopher was a real person to Gran not just a shadow or whatever he is now. Also I don't think Christopher would like it which seems a silly thing to think. Once I had a toy rabbit I used to take to bed. I took it for a walk one day and I saw a boy from school and I dropped Sebastian, that was his name, the rabbit, not the boy, over the wall of a house so Jack, who was the boy wouldn't see me with a toy rabbit. I had to go back for it later and it was stuck in a holly bush and quite hard to get out. I felt as though I'd betrayed him like Judas Iscariot betrayed Jesus, or is that being blasphemous? Then I have another idea. What if instead of me seeing Christopher and thinking no one else can, Gran can see him but she doesn't think anyone else can so she pretends he isn't there either. Like when you tell someone a secret and they just say everyone knows that. When I said to Sophe, 'D'you think Miss Groves is pregnant?' She said, 'Like only for the last nine months.'

Gran's friend Wendy who was here the other day comes to go blackberrying! Sophe rings and says she's going to Spain. I say, 'I'm going blackberrying,' she says, it's bad enough to say what Nans say. I don't have to do what Nan's do.

Gran and Wendy spend some time discussing what to put the blackberries in. It seems they used to use bowls or punnets when they were young. They've known each other since George VI was king. I know that because they talk about burning down the bramble bushes to go on a procession for the coronation. I suppose the coronation was like the millennium, Street parties and dancing on village greens. I quite like to think of picking blackberries. When I was in year two our school was a hundred years old. We had to dress up like when the first children came, in smocks and carrying slates which were like individual blackboards. Like having your own laptop Mr. Allan said. We were supposed to take something of the time and I couldn't think of anything. Nathan came with his lunch wrapped up in a red and white spotted handkerchief on a stick which was totally over the top said Sophe. I could have taken a basket of blackberries! Well if it was blackberry time. It wasn't but I expect you could get frozen ones in Tescos.

Gran picks up a polythene bag but Wendy says they'll go all squashy. Gran picks up a glass bowl which Wendy says it too heavy, its like Little Red Riding Hood choosing her porridge. In the end they get a couple of plastic boxes with lids which Wendy says are 'just right' and we really do set off. Wendy has a car and knows where the best ones grow which isn't the prettiest place, not on a field. Its by the Park and Ride which Wendy says is useful for the car anyway.

Gran asks Wendy how her mother is. I'm surprised she's still got a mother.

'She's completely lost it, she's started talking to Harry,'

Harry is Wendy's father apparently and he's been dead for twenty years.

'More dotty than com,' she says and I think of what people would say if I told them about talking to Christopher. I mean I'm not even an old woman. Perhaps I've got a premature ageing disease, which is a horrible thought.

'I always thought your Mum had a sixth sense,' says Gran. A sixth sense sounded better, more like a witch than someone with Alzheimer's.

Is this the moment to introduce my ghost?

'I think I've got a sixth sense.' I say for a start. Gran laughs and Wendy says, wait till you've developed the other five. I can only think of four till I scratch myself on a bramble and remember the fifth. I give a shout.

'Have you been stung?' I show them my scratch.

'Its only a scratch,' says Gran.

'But it's a classic,' says Wendy. It is a classic. It's skagged across my arm in staggered blood marks. It is a perfect scratch. If I was in a police enquiry and said I'd got it picking blackberries they'd know I was telling the truth. Then I realise she meant 'Its only a scratch,' is a classic. The expression I mean like what Nan's say. I suppose they're laughing at me because they got scratched all the time when they were girls. Wendy's says about how once their mother told them not to go in the sea when they went to Weymouth because she had a premonition someone was going to drown and someone had drowned. A boy in a dinghy who'd floated out to sea. They'd found the dinghy with no one in it. Which I suppose was to explain to me what a sixth sense was. It sounded scary.

'Did they find the body?' asked Gran but later as though she'd been thinking about it or knew him. Wendy said they hadn't known about it till it was in the papers the next day, her mother read it out and said, I told you so. She said it must have been when they were in the amusements or feeding the swans, which made it sound worse as if they could have saved him if they'd listened like knowing the lottery numbers and not bothering to buy a ticket. And I forgot it all happened before I was born and if he had been saved he might have died by now or be sixty five.

Gran and Wendy pick much faster than me. Well they had had more practice. Some of the blackberries were ripe some were hard and red and some still in flower and there were butterflies on the flowers like it was spring and summer and autumn all rolled into one which seemed to belong to a magic world. There were flies too and wasps so it was mostly summer.

'Its hard to find a perfect blackberry,' I say.

'Like pigeon's feet, you rarely find a pigeon with perfect feet,' Gran says. I thought of when we were in Wells. Then a bird came down and picked a blackberry, it wasn't a pigeon, it was a blackbird with a bright orange beak. I felt like a country girl.

When we'd filled the containers Wendy drove us to a garden centre to have a toasted teacake and a cup of tea and a slice of lemon drizzle cake. Which at least was what 'What Nans do now,' rather than 'What Nan's did then.' Gran bought a tree. A little one, with red leaves so thin they shivered in the wind. It looked foreign, or like in a Chelsea flower show on television with stones round it and its own pond.

'An Acer.' says Gran.

'A Maple,' says Wendy.

'Whats in a name,' says Gran. Wendy said she liked my name, Matilda because it was an old name. She said her name was a new one but it didn't sound very new to me, and it couldn't be very new if it was hers. I didn't say this. She said it was made up by James Barrie who wrote Peter Pan. It was the first Wendy because he knew a little girl with a lisp who said, 'Be my fwendy.' She died when she was six, the girl I mean who's real name was Margaret.

'Is that why he wrote about a boy who never grew up?' Asks Gran.

'No that was because he had a brother who died when he was fourteen,' and then she stopped herself and said, 'Sorry,' I suppose she must have known about Christopher if she went picking blackberries with Gran when they were girls. Christopher might have gone with them. She said Peter Pan and the lost boys were based on some real boys who all died young.

'In the war?' asked Gran but I don't know which one. Wendy said one of them drowned swimming, at school or university.

'Never mind I expect the crocodile ate them all in the end,' said Gran.

I thought of the little girl saying, 'be my fwendy,' to a man and being called Wendy in a story but not knowing about it. Not like Alice in Wonderland who's real name was Alice Liddell, and did know. I liked the thought of James Barrie's brother turning into Peter Pan and flying around in a book. It made me think of Christopher again. I wanted him to be there, to tell him. But I didn't see him. That's the trouble with ghosts they never appear when you want them and I did a little shivery laugh.

'Who's walked over your grave?' asked Wendy which made it sound like she might have inherited her mother's sixth sense.

'How old is your mother?' I asked.

'Ninety two,' and I said about Mrs. Woolley who learnt something new every day.

'My mother forgets something new every day,' Wendy laughed.

We went back and planted the tree in the garden and I saw Christopher throwing a cricket ball along the side of the path where we planted the tree.

'There used to be a laburnum tree here,'

'Is that to replace it.' I asked.

She said the Laburnum had yellow flowers, and nearly every garden had one and the seeds were poisonous but we didn't know that then,' said Gran. I wondered if Christopher had eaten the seeds and died of Laburnum seed poisoning.

'We used it like stumps,' said Gran

'Stumps?'

'Yes we played cricket, well mostly my brother and the boys next door. Jackie wouldn't play and I wasn't very good.'

We rang the hospital who said Ed was doing very well before we rang Mum who was almost crying with relief. I felt pleased too and then guilty because I hadn't been thinking about Ed. He might have died while I was seeing an apparition of a boy who died half a century ago. Then Gran said something to Grandad about not being out of the woods yet which sounded ominous and I thought of Wendy's mother with her sixth sense. An old country witch foreseeing a death when everyone else thought it was safe to go back in the woods.

I ring Sophe who's in Spain. I'd forgotten and I imagined her back at home She actually answers her mobile by saying, 'Ole.'

I tell her about the party which already seemed a long time ago and now Sophe was a long way away and only interested in Spain and a Spanish waiter who'd called her an English rose. She starts to speak in Spanish again. I don't mention the blackberries being like something out of Dickens or even Ed.

The next day its raining. I ring Ed and say about the blackberries to him as I thought he'd think that was OK in an organic way and say how he would be better now and back at school worse luck. I actually say, 'worse luck' like a person in an Enid Blyton book though I havn't read any Enid Blyton books so I don't know if they do.

'You've been down South too long.' Ed likes school and I quite like it. Ed didn't say much and I thought perhaps he's too ill to talk. I mean when you can't see someone it's hard to imagine how desperate they are. When the people on their mobile phones were falling out of the Twin Towers I don't expect the people getting the calls saying, 'I love you,' realised just how bad things were. Not unless they were watching the telly at the same time.

Ed said, 'He's dead.' And his voice sounds dead too. I thought of Christopher as if Ed knew I'd seen him and was telling me something I already knew which wasn't like Ed.

'Who?'

'Leo.' I'd forgotten Leo, the boy in hospital.

'He was really good at chess,' he says as though it might be written on his gravestone. Playing chess the only thing he hadn't missed. Ed isn't crying. Ed doesn't cry but he might as well be.

'Why him?' He said as though he'd been picked on unfairly. As though there was a death decider. I just think as long as it isn't Ed and I can't feel sad about Leo though I feel I ought to. It was more like he was James Barrie's brother who he turned into Peter Pan. I think of saying how he'll be like Peter Pan. But being like Peter Pan doesn't sound a very good thing anymore.

Mum comes on and says Ed's very tired she sounds very tired herself. I feel like I'm in a different country with a different culture. Like I'm safe while they are at war.

CHAPTER ELEVEN

Next day there's a lot of activity next door as Failand and Kate are going to a pony club thing. They're even wearing jodpurs. Hamish is shouting to go with them, in the end they take him and Maria waves from the door looking pleased. Gran says something about frightening the horses. I think she means Hamish. Toby is driving.

'They look like an ideal family.' I say feeling jealous, not that I want to go but wishing I wanted to go. Well that I want to go somewhere or that I'd been asked.

'You shouldn't judge a book by its cover,' says Gran.

'Why is she really a wicked stepmother going to drive them into the lake?' Then she tells me about how they first came to live here after Miles and Failand's Dad had left them for Paris and his new girlfriend. How Nina had just married Toby, who's Grandfather, Charlie still lived there and how pleased she was to be having another baby and how upset they'd been when Hamish………. well turned out to be Hamish I suppose. It made me look like I don't understand other people's problems. Like I didn't understand Ed who's friend was dead and had to think he might die himself. I feel annoyed with Gran as I'd forgotten about Toby not being their Dad and Hamish only being their half brother and though one's not supposed to say it Hamish must have been a shock. Well till they got used to him. I think they wouldn't have known at first, been all pleased with him, the new baby, his blonde hair and blue eyes asleep in his cot. Till he woke up.

'Hamish didn't say his first word till he was three,' she says.

'A lot of people don't speak till they're three.' I say. I'm not really sure but it doesn't sound that bad.

'But he didn't say another till he was four,' we both laugh.

'Nobody's perfect,' says Grandad coming in from the garden. And it seems alright about Hamish like in a Nativity play, not everyone can be Mary or Joseph, someone's got to be a shepherd or even a sheep. Marley start to purr he's sitting on my lap, its the first time he's done that, I stroke him and feel like person who's kind to animals at least.

'Is there anywhere you want to go?' asks Grandad as if we could go anywhere in the world. I think of turning up in Spain and surprising Sophe. He's got what he calls a courtesy car off the garage, something to do with insurance and wants to try it out. Maybe he thinks I'm upset about not being asked to go to the Pony club thing but I've forgotten it already.

'In striking distance,' Grandad adds as though he's read my mind about Spain.

'Cheddar,' I suggest because it's a place I'd heard of and seen pictures of but never been. There's a silence as though I've said something no one wants to hear. I couldn't think what could be wrong with Cheddar. Did it mean something else, apart from cheese and caves?

'Second choice?' says Grandad but I couldn't think of anywhere except Weston where we always went when we came to stay. There was Lyme Regis of course when me and Ed had looked for fossils like Mary Anning who'd found a kind f dinosaur and only found ammonites anyway but that wasn't in striking distance.

'We can go to Cheddar if you want to,' says Gran but like she didn't want to.

'I just saw a picture of this gorge in the pamphlet of where to go in the West Country, it wasn't that special.' I could see they weren't keen on Cheddar. I mean it wasn't as though they didn't eat cheese. I could understand a vegetarian not wanting to go to a beef ranch.

'If it's a gorge you're after we can go to the suspension bridge,' says Grandad as though he'd found a way out. I didn't think the suspension bridge was something you'd go to. More cross over and Gran said the same.

'We could go to Clifton.'

We do go across the suspension bridge which is more famous than Cheddar but I'd seen it. Its was built by someone called Isambard Kingdom Brunel, said Gran which sounded like he'd been named after a ship or a tunnel himself.

'He was a French refugee.'

'He didn't actually build it himself, and he wasn't a French refugee he was the son of a French refugee,' said Grandad as if he was getting back at her for Pero's bridge.

'Well at least he designed it.'

He'd also designed Temple Meads which is the train station and an iron ship called the S.S. Great Britain which is still here along the river, they brought it back from somewhere, the Falklands I think. I don't know where the Falklands are or why it was there. It was before the Falklands war which was before I was born. We went on it once Ed wanted to. It's a big ship where they used to have dinners and dances like on the Titanic. But I couldn't really imagine going on it. On a voyage I mean like to New York or somewhere and getting dressed up and going down to dinner. It looked quite grand but not that clean as if a rat might run across the dinner table. I was surprised people dressed up to go on a ship, dressed up like going to a wedding I mean, not like a sailor, or in a sou-wester.

'A busy man,' says Grandad.

Isambard died in 1859 it said on a plaque. That was before the bridge was built so he never saw it. It's impressive going over and looking down on the river which is grey and winding like in an aerial picture. The river's in a gorge and you can imagine it going out to sea like rivers are supposed to do because you can see it bending along in a purposeful way. But really the bridge looks better looking up at it like when we're going into town. Especially when there was a high tide with little ducks swimming across as though they had too far to go to get to the other side. I was sorry Isambard hadn't seen it.

Gran must be been thinking the same because she says, 'It would be worth a resurrection.' I suppose it would be like Charles Dickens seeing his books being on television, Isambard seeing cars going over his bridge. Christopher must have gone across? It looks like something he'd build a model of.

We have tapas in a Clifton wine bar and look at shoes while Grandad goes to a Pub with the crossword. Gran buys some with laces. I try some on but I don't like to buy shoes without Sophe's approval. Then we drive round the downs to look for peregrine falcons which we don't see, only seagulls and crows but it looks like a good place to nest if you were a bird of prey. There's lots of cars parked.

'Whats on?'

Gran says there might be a circus or a flower show but there isn't. The cars are for the Zoo. We go past the Zoo, there's a queue for the Zoo. I asked if we can go, the queue makes it exciting, like somewhere people want to be.

'If you like, after all we are on holiday,' she says like we'd just arrived in a different country. I did like. Grandad doesn't look too happy saying they'd had to get rid of the big cats and elephants because of animal correctness and now it was bats and rats because it wasn't easy to offend a rat though it soon would be. We go in anyway and there are monkeys and a gorilla enclosure and snakes in interesting cases like moonscapes or something artists might make with old bits of wood they might pick up on the beach or buy at a garden centre.

Gran tells us about when she came to the Zoo sort of longer ago than a giant tortoise. There was an elephant named Rosie you could have rides on.

'I can just see Rosie now,' she says, 'plodding along in front of the big cats cages, and me and Jackie had a ride on her back, well I think we did, there's a photograph somewhere.'

'What about your brother?' I say bravely wanting Christopher to have had an elephant ride.

'Oh he would have been too young,' says Gran quickly, 'of course you wouldn't be able to ride on an elephant now. An elephant wasn't so sensitive when we were children.'

'Quiz team Roger said his Auntie Flo worked at the Zoo and when Rosie died they had to cut her up because she was too big to fit on the lorry and everyone was crying,' Grandad says, and I wish he hadn't told us that story. I preferred Gran's.

'A woman wouldn't have been an elephant keeper then.' I don't think Gran wants to believe him.

'She was a waitress,' says Grandad. 'she worked in the café,' making it sound true.

'How did they get her in then?' asks Gran as though she's found a loophole in his story.

'I expect she walked.'

'In India they make them carry logs,' I say but I'm not sure if they still do, though it would be better than being in a circus or even a Zoo. Carrying logs is an elephant kind of job. You usually see African elephants on television just being elephants, well sometimes they get killed for their tusks. There was a dead one on television that had died of thirst who looked deflated, like an elephant bag with nothing in it. Grandad says when my Dad was a boy and they brought him here, there was a new elephant called Wendy. The keeper brought her out for a walk to meet the children but the children were all playing on the climbing frames and didn't seem very interested and he'd been embarrassed for Wendy. He thought she'd sooner be giving rides than being ignored in favour of a swing or a spider. I thought of the girl who said be my 'fwendy' and how she didn't know an elephant was called after her. But she didn't know a character in a book was called after her. She wasn't even called Wendy herself. I thought of her standing by her gate as James Barrie went by. There are a lot of children playing in the adventure park today. High up on rope ladders.

'Agile as monkeys,' says Gran looking up enviously.

'Perhaps they're trying to compensate for their lack of monkeys,' says Grandad. A bit further on there's a real monkey a black one with a white beard who comes swinging towards us on his rope like a cartoon.

'OK they weren't as agile as monkeys,' concedes Gran.

'No contest.' Grandad agrees.

We go underground to watch the seals, they have this way of moving like peaceful bombs. Grandad says they make him want to go to sleep and he does fall asleep on a seat in the sun by big yellow flowers. A peacock fans out its tail but it doesn't look so good when it turns round.

'All front, like a fashion shot,' says Gran. It feels like a foreign land with the big flowers and the sound of monkeys and screeching birds.

'La Grande Jatte,' says Gran.

'Didn't know you spoke French Jen,' says Grandad waking up. Gran says it was a the name of a French painting of people by a river and one of them had a monkey. There weren't actually any monkey's on the lawn but you could have got hold of one quite easily. Well if you were a famous painter and put in a special request. We go on past the flamingos who looked like tall pink swans.

'Black underwear very Oo la la,' says Grandad as one of them shook out it's feathers and they were black underneath.

'You'd think it'd show through,' says Gran as though he was serious.

There was a lion but he didn't look very happy.

'Out of place almost,' says Gran.

'Not like when you were a girl,' says Grandad a bit sarcastically.

'Yes a lion had a bit or presence then. Now photography's so good they look better on television.'

'They smell better too,' says Grandad.

A girl is trying to annoy the lion who's pacing up and down like waiting for somebody but then he suddenly turns round and roars at the girl who jumps back looking scared. Well she has her face painted like a tiger so it's hard to tell if she looks scared or just scary. No wonder the lion roared. She's one of those children who can't keep still, we've got them in our class. She's too young for our class, more year three or four.

'Wouldn't like to meet him in a jungle clearing,' says Gran.

' Jungle clearing it 'aint,' says Grandad though it is big cage with a ball for him to play with if he likes. The lion yawns as if he agrees. The lion looks like a big cat. I know that's what lions are called but he actually looks like Marley and Spider, the same expression on his face. But more like Marley because they're more the same colour. I think of Spider and feel quite homesick I wonder if she's missing me but I don't think cats do. Though she does look out of the window when I come home from school, as though she's been waiting. And she notices everything. When she was a kitten and me and Dad took her to the vet's to get her spayed the vet said to have her chipped which we did, when we got back and told Mum all pleased with ourselves she said, 'Why?' Dad said. 'In case she gets lost,' said Dad. 'Cats come back,' she said.

I wonder if this lion would come back if he got out of his cage, if he thinks this is home?

'He's never seen a jungle clearing,' says a black man pointing to a label that says: Born in the Gardens.

'Have you?' Asks Grandad and I think the man might be offended or laugh at him like black people do as though white people thought they were born in the jungle. I don't, unless they were of course. I mean there is still a jungle isn't there? Or is it called something else. A rain forest say. Were you born in a rain forest would sound OK unless someone thought you were saying they were wet.

'Not me mate, I was born in the gardens too,' says the man but he's still laughing. I suppose he means he was born here, in Bristol. He's got a Bristol accent.

Then he says, 'Come on Jasmine. That's a real lion,' to the girl as though she'd thought it was a toy.

'Your daughter?' asks Grandad.

'My grand daughter,' says the man sounding pleased all the same. He does look a lot younger than Gran and Grandad. I expect he is.

We see them again outside the café. Jasmine's catching wasps in a coke can. Grandad starts chatting to the man who's name is Michael Jackson. He says he was

Michael Jackson first and Michael Jackson was probably named after him and I expect he's said this a few times. Grandad's name is Michael too. When they'd got over that they start talking about cricket and Gran closes her eyes like the Slow Loris asleep in a tree. When we went by Gran said, 'When I come back I'll come back as a Slow Loris.' Being asleep makes her look not dead so much as old. There's dark cloud over the sun and I feel threatened.

'Come with me, lets get a balloon,' says Jasmine. There was a boy at the next table with a parrot balloon but he was only about five. I look at Gran and Grandad and think how much older than Jasmine's Grandfather they look and I feel old myself compared with Jasmine. Too old for Parrot balloons. Gran's hair is brown on top but quite grey at the roots. Jasmine catches hold of my hand in a friendly trusting kind of way so I follow her into the insect house. It's dark and we watch the spiders and things that are hard to see with all their camouflage. There are tiny frogs in bright colours like graphics in a computer game. Jasmine is trying to make them hop through the glass. I mean she taps the glass to make them hop inside their case. Not get out, more touch screen.

'They've never seen a rain forest,' I say but it doesn't seem to matter as they're so small the glass case would seem like a rain forest to them. I found a lizard looking like piece of rock and go to show Jasmine as she feels like my little sister which I quite like the thought of, having a little sister to show things to though I can't imagine my mother having another baby. I don't think I'd want one for real. Then I can't see her anywhere. I know it's dark and she's black, well not black like her granddad more golden brown and wearing a yellow dress as bright as the frogs. She should be easy to find because she's as jumpy as a frog and thats when you see the lizards, when they move. I feel quite ecological. Anyway I'm not supposed to be looking after her. I hadn't met her half an hour ago and now I feel like she's my responsibility. It's like with Hamish, not that she's got a disability or anything, more like one of those extra bouncy balls. The insect house has an exit, which isn't where we'd come in and I don't know where I am. There's no one to ask only some teenage Japanese girls taking photographs and laughing in an oriental way. I think they might be laughing at our Zoo with its little frogs because they eat whales in Japan.

When I get out I can't find the café either. There's a pond but not the one with the sea lions in, just a big pond with lots of different kinds of ducks. There's some Prairie Rats who like standing up, like poodles, but aren't as famous as Meercats. These are eating a dead magpie which seems sinister. I don't know if that's their dinner, or if they've caught it, or it just died there. They don't look particularly carnivorous but Magpies like to eat dead things so perhaps it serves them right. I go past the gorilla park and wonder if she's got in because I remember something on television where a gorilla saves a boy who fell into his pit. What if Jasmine's had seen the same programme and is expecting too much of gorillas? Not that this one's in a pit just a gorilla garden so it might have a gate. I can only see one gorilla and he's asleep. I'm lost, though there are lots of signposts, if Ed was here he's follow the signposts. He might even get a map. But the signposts point to the different animals not Gran or Jasmine.

There's another door which I thought Jasmine might have gone through, it's full of nocturnal animals and quite interesting. You could use it to make a horror film. I am beginning to feel I'm in a horror film as something jumped towards me like marsupials do staring at me with bright eyes like it was trying to put a spell on me.

A man standing by the cage starts explaining them to me. Where they come from and about evolution and everything and I think of the Just So stories like, 'How did the giraffe get its name?' Or was it it's neck? And that makes me think of school and I think he's probably a teacher. I wish he'd shut up because sometimes I just like to look at things, not know about them.

'Are you on your own?' he asks and I went to tell him about losing Jasmine and then I suddenly feel afraid. I think of the girl saying, 'be my fwendy' and how you wouldn't say that now and what if he was a paedophile and if he sexually assaulted me in the dark. Sophe would say I'd been stupid to talk to a man alone in a nocturnal house.

'Is Jasmine your sister?' he has a nice voice. I wish Ed was here though he isn't really the kind of brother to rescue you from a paedophile more likely to say I was prejudiced.

'There's my Dad,' I say just so I could get away. He said he couldn't see him.

'Thats because he's black,' I say thinking of Jasmine's Grandad who wouldn't show up much in a nocturnal house.

'What did you say?' the man sounded shocked. He probably is a teacher, anyway not a paedophile anymore than Clocker Wallace but it wouldn't matter he just wouldn't have a 'fwendy.'

I ran then. When I got outside there was Jasmine being handed an ice cream by a man with a shaved head and two silver studs on his lip wearing a red football shirt. I thought he was abducting her as she's very friendly and would probably talk to anyone.

I grabbed her and knocked the ice cream onto the ground. I mean that was an accident, the ice cream. I didn't think it was drugged or anything, just a bribe.

'What the hell,' he said. No he said worse than that but this is for school. Jasmine looked annoyed too.

'You mustn't take ice cream from strangers,' I say severely, maybe the man would think I was her step sister.

'I'm only her bloody Dad,' he said instead but he didn't sound so cross. I looked at Jasmine who said he was. Her dad I mean.

'I'm sorry,' I said, 'I didn't think.'

'I know what you thought,' he said. Did he think I though he was a paedophile or that he wasn't her father because he was white. I did in a way because most mixed race girls I know have white mothers and black fathers. It was impossible to move on like one of those games Ed plays. I can never get to the next level. Si I started crying. I don't know why but once I started I couldn't stop.

Jasmine put her arm round me like she was the big sister and the man says. 'Come on we'll find your Mum,'

'My Mum's not here,' I say which makes her sound dead or divorced and that made me cry more because I almost believed it myself.

'What's going on?' Grandad appeared like a good fairy at a christening.

I was relieved at first then afraid he was going to accuse Jasmine's Dad of abducting both of us. Then a black woman with a little boy who looked like Jasmine, well he didn't have his face painted but it was the same shade of brown. He was only about two or three but looking round solemnly like someone who was going to have to write it all up afterwards. Anyway they look like a family and a seagull swooped down and picked up the ice cream, rather neatly I thought.

'Well that clears that up,' said Grandad and I don't know if he meant the ice cream or who was who.

I went back to the café with Grandad. Gran was still asleep.

'Where d'you find a tortoise with no legs?' asked Grandad.

'I don't know,'

'Where you left her,' and I realised he meant Gran not the tortoise at the Zoo which was very big and very old and probably dated back to the origin of the species. I'm not quite sure what that is but I like the sound of it and it seemed appropriate as Mrs. James would say.

'Don't mention going AWOL to your Gran, she's a bit sensitive, she lost her brother,' says Grandad as though that explained a lot but it didn't tell me much except that Christopher must have been missing before he was dead. I didn't know what AWOL means either but I suppose it means something like truanting. Grandad told the other Michael we'd met his family by the nocturnal house. He said he knew he'd just texted them and he was meeting them by the gorilla enclosure which seemed too easy somehow.

Gran woke up embarrassed at having been asleep. The sky had gone all dark like a tropical rainstorm was going to fall on the tropical plants and animals. I bought a card for Ed of lemurs, though we'd missed the lemurs. I liked the way their tails dangled down on the post card. Gran bought a black and white post card of Alfred, a gorilla who died in 1948. She said he was stuffed in the museum, which seemed like a kind of afterlife. So did the postcard and there was a statue of his head. Alfred's I mean. He was iconic. It was raining really hard by now and it was all muddy by the time we got back to the car.

'Look a peregrine falcon,' said Grandad pointing up at some biggish bird of prey and he seemed more excited than by all the animals in the Zoo.

I didn't see Christopher in my room that night. I dreamed Marley the cat was asleep on the basket chair and put out his paw, straight out like cat's do. When I went to stroke him he turned into the lion at the Zoo and roared at me and I woke up. I had a funny feeling in my legs, a feeling of fear, though the real lion hadn't seemed frightening. Well he was in a cage. I thought the man in the nocturnal house only seemed frightening because he was in the dark. I wanted to go to the bathroom. There seemed to be a noise downstairs I wondered if there was a burglar. There was a ghostly sort of light. I crept down and looked into the room and there was Gran sat on the chair watching night time television. It was an Open University history programme about Henry VIII and his wives who got beheaded. Not all of them I know but it was seriously grim. Christopher was there playing with a toy plane but more shadowy than usual, more like a ghost. Perhaps he was fading away. Gran jumped when she saw me.

'I couldn't sleep,' she said, 'I slept too long at the Zoo,' which sounded like a song. Actually she didn't sound right, and she didn't look right. She looked older in her dressing gown but it was more than that. Then I realised some of her teeth were missing, like they'd been blacked out on a poster. I think Gran realised too because she got up very suddenly and went into the kitchen to put the kettle on. I felt sorry for Gran and wanted to put the clock back as they say. I thought of pushing the hands of Big Ben back till Gran was young again and in the room with Christopher and the television wasn't here, or only black and white. But then I wouldn't be here either and it seems like we all had to take our turns at being alive or on the clock, like having your turn in a game.

Gran came back in and she looked like herself again. We both felt embarrassed. I mean though you know about old people having dentures and see adverts for them on television its not the same as seeing them. Its like hearing someone wets the bed. It might not mean much unless you went camping with them. I told her about my dream and she made us some hot chocolate and we sat there like we were waiting for someone to come home form the sea. Or an old married couple. Well I can't imagine being married, not even to Miles. Certainly not to Miles. Miles coming home and playing his guitar and reading the papers and a child playing a game no one's thought of yet. I don't think so. Will we have papers by then or just one big screen with everything on? We'd be able to order our food, watch the news, adjust the heat or turn on an artificial wind if global warming had really taken off.

It was still raining the next day. I woke up late and watched the raindrops on the window joining up like snow. Gran was pleased for her little red tree which looked more English in the rain.

'Why don't you ask Failand over?' but I didn't know what I'd do with Failand. It wasn't like Sophe.

'I bet it isn't raining in Spain.'

'Depends what part,' says Gran. 'The rain in Spain falls mainly on the plain,' which she thought was funny. I write my card to Ed. 'We went to the Zoo but didn't see the lemurs though I'm sure they were there.' Which seems a waste of space but I didn't want to waste the whole card. Gran says I could send the Alfred the gorilla card but I thought of Alfred being dead and stuffed in the museum and Ed's friend being dead. I'd forgotten that so I put sorry about Leo. I want to say I'm sure he's there somewhere, like the lemurs, but it didn't sound right turning him into a stripy tailed bush baby on a postcard as though death was camouflage. But I don't think he is, not like Christopher. There was this poem we did at school when we had Kirsty, a student teacher. It was by John Keats who died quite young. "Time you old Gypsy man will you not stay, put up your caravan just for one day?" Kirsty asked me what I thought he meant. I didn't answer because I'd turned over the pages in the book and found a poem about a woman who's brothers cut off her boyfriend's head and she kept it in a pot of Basil. Basil the herb, it was growing out of his head. How ghoulish is that?

Nathan put his hand up. He said he thought it was because he wanted time to stop for a while so he could finish the crossword. His Mum said his Dad wasted too much time doing crosswords and when he died they'd send him back to do extra time to get some work done. We all laughed but Kirsty wasn't happy. Then I think what if Ed had a relapse. What if he just isn't there when I go back. What if his time has run out.

I put a first class stamp on the card to hurry it up in case this really is the last post and go out in the rain to the red box on the corner. It has VR on it which mean it was built when Queen Victoria was queen. I feel like John Keats wanting time to park up. The rain's made everything feel sad. Well except for the little red tree and ducks of course. Ed hadn't known Leo very long. Would I be sad if Failand falls off her horse and got killed. I try to feel upset about it but I cant. Maybe I don't care. But it hasn't happened so I can't tell.

Gran asks if I want to do some painting, she's got all this painting stuff from an art class she goes to with a woman called Linda who I haven't met. She has some pictures she's painted. One of Marley sat up and one of Marley lying down. There's one of Crosby, a dead dog. I remember Crosby, a brown spaniel. There's a big one of trees in Ashton Court with hot air balloons going up that won a prize in a flower show. I think the best one is of Grandad asleep in the chair. I paint the little red tree out of the window. Then I put some lemurs in it, like the ones on the postcard. At one point I see Christopher sitting in the chair as though he's posing for us. It's obvious Gran isn't aware him as she's painting some pears she's put on a plate on the table. I think if I paint Christopher into my painting will he disappear like magic writing. Then I think what if I just take his photograph. Will it come out? It seems creepy, like those girls who pretended they'd seen fairies. People really believed they were fairies but they'd just cut them out of a book and put them in the woods and taken their photographs. You couldn't do that today, people would know. I carry on painting I know Christopher would realise I couldn't talk to him when Gran was there. It looks quite good when it's finished and Gran glues it onto some card so it looks like a proper picture.

Mum rings later and says Ed was depressed on account of his friend dying. She says Dad would come and fetch me if Gran was fed up with looking after me. She doesn't ask what I want but I expect she doesn't like to in case I say I'm fed up in front of Gran. She does say she's missing me but then she says about a posh Pub where they'd gone out to dinner with some people they'd met at the hospital. Really nice people who's daughter Holly is ill too, such a pretty girl and so brave. They've moved into a hospital existence and I'm not part of it. I don't mean I'm jealous of Ed because he's getting all the attention. A girl said that to me at school. Like I'd be jealous of my brother having leukaemia. How sick is that? I know Mum and Dad do go on about his blood count and a lot which I think gets on Ed's nerves more than mine. She says he's in isolation because he mustn't catch anything because his immune system is low. I'm not sure what an immune system is. I ask Gran.

'It means he's vulnerable to infection he couldn't fight off the littlest germ?' she says as though I was about five. My fault for asking. I remember when me and Ed were sort of fighting on the beach, when he was trying to push me in the water to make me swim and I was screaming. Dad said, 'leave her alone, its not fair she's younger than you,' Ed said, 'It's not supposed to be fair. Its the survival of the fittest.' Ed did seem so

111

much older and stronger than me then. Now I think of him in isolation not being able to fight off the littlest germ.

CHAPTER TWELVE

When Grandad comes in from work there's a rainbow. Gran says how once she'd believed there was a pot of gold at the end of a rainbow and she'd gone to find it but it moved away like the horizon, but now she was fed up with staying in and she'd like to go and have another try.

'Lets go down the Duke,' says Grandad. 'there's a good band on tonight.'

I know Gran and Grandad are a couple of old jazzers as Dad calls them. Dad says he was brought up on jazz pubs himself. We often send Grandad birthday cards with black and white photos of dead musicians. There's a trumpeter called Louis Armstrong and a woman singer called Ella, but it was all on the cards. I never thought of them as actually going to a jazz club. I'm not much into music as you might have guessed by now and never really thought what jazz was. I mixed it up with folk singing or blues, something American anyway. But it was ages ago, before the war, before Elvis, like they were all dead now, not just Louis Armstrong. I can see why people fancied Elvis, well when he was young and so were Gran and Grandad.

'Not Mattie's cup of tea,' said Gran but I quite liked the idea of a jazz club, all dark and spooky with someone like Louis Armstrong who I had seen on television playing in a big band.

'Why don't you ask Failand,' says Grandad, 'or wouldn't you girls think it was cool.'

'We don't say cool anymore,' I say.

I felt embarrassed about asking Failand to come to a jazz pub with two old people. Then she rang me saying she was bored, by the rain and not going riding and did I want to come over. So I did say it.

'D'you want to come to a jazz Pub?'

'Cool,' she said.

By the time we left the rain had gone off and it was quite sunny in an evening sort of way. There was a field full of camper vans with people sat outside drinking tea as if something was about to happen. Like the Queen or a celebrity was on their way.

'Is it a caravan boot sale?' I ask as I don't think the Queen is coming.

'Its the balloon festival, the balloon festival is coming, they said together as if everybody knew. Well everyone except me. There were posters I hadn't noticed before, it was international apparently. I know they've got a lot of balloons round here but it seemed funny the field turning into a camp site and everyone getting ready for an event. I almost expected the sea to be over the wall but I knew it was Ashton Court where we'd gone riding. You could see tents going up among the tall grasses, the grass was brown like a foreign country. But there was a church behind the camping field which definitely made it look like a village, though not a village green.

'It's seasonal,' explained Grandad, 'They have lambs in January, then the cows come out to graze, then they let it lie fallow and clean itself up for the camper vans then back to cows and a bit of silage.'

The jazz pub's in a cobbled road called King Street with a theatre and a really old Pub like Queen Elizabeth the first might have slept there. I don't think she did but she did come to Bristol and rode on a white horse and said about a church which is on the way to Isambard's station. She said it was the fairest in the land, the church. Anyway this old looking Pub's called the Llandoger Trow and its got black and white beams and things which is what I call Elizabethan like Shakespeare might have had a play on here. The square was full of people who looked like they might have watched it. Gran said it had only been cobbled recently it used to be a through road. The Llandoger Trow isn't the one with the jazz in it but everyone's sitting outside so it's the one you see most as it's opposite the jazz Pub which has an inn sign with a piano player on. Robinson Crusoe was here or whoever wrote it. Its hardly a desert island but there is a river with loads of swans. What I notice most is how old the people are.

'It's like a pensioner's party,' says Failand and I feel responsible. She is right its like a Coronation, street reunion. The real coronation I mean not the soap. Well I don't suppose they're any older than Gran and Grandad, its probably seeing them all together.

'Its better when the students come back,' says Gran as though she felt she should apologise too. Like the students would liven it up for us. I remember Abe saying jazz was black people's music. It looks more like old people's music. The band is all old white men. But when they're playing they look special in a musician kind of way and you can almost believe they were young once, like if they came on television like the Beatles and they showed pictures of them when they were young, but I don't suppose they're famous enough for that. The trumpeter is a short fat man with a red face and a Father Christmas beard. Not exactly Louis Armstrong but he looks quite good puffing away. In the interval they just look like ordinary old men and Grandad is talking to them about cricket and introduces me to the piano player who asks me if I'm interested in music as they need some young blood.

'No,' I say which sounds a bit rude but I'm not, interested in music that is.

'How about you ?' to Failand who says she sings. That she used to have lessons and her teacher said she had perfect pitch but she'd given it up. Which sounds worse as though someone showed you their very best present and you say you had one of those but you threw it away.

The seagulls are lit up. I don't mean for real like the green trees that are lit up like pantomime trees, a gel coloured green. But lit up by accident as the lights catch them, they become pure white then disappear as they fly out to the river. I think of Christopher. Has he just come into a sort of special light that makes him visible and when he goes outside it he disappears.

We're sitting on silver chairs and Failand says its like Paris where her real Dad lives and she goes over on Eurostar to see him with Miles. She makes going to Paris sound like something you do every day and having two Dad's as better than one. So I stop feeling sorry for her about her Dad going off with his French girlfriend. I still can't imagine my Dad leaving, even when Mum and dad having a row, which they do. Then she says they've had a baby, her Dad and the French woman. I think she may have two half brothers.

'Whats its name?' I ask to find out what sex it is.

'Something unpronounceable,' she says as if she isn't interested. French I suppose, though I don't think of French names as being unpronounceable, more two joined together like Marie-Claire or Jean-Paul.

'French?' I say, as it now seems important.

'More Double Dutch,' and we both find this funny.

The band starts playing and Grandad goes in to get a drink and Gran's talking to a woman she knows who's going to sing in a minute who looks too old to be a singer though I know old people do sing. I am surprised when she sings she sounds like somebody else, like a fat black woman though she's thin and white.

'She's not bad,' says Failand as though she's an expert. Maybe she is?

'He died in my arms, with his head on my lap,' the singer is saying afterwards talking to Gran and I think she's talking about her husband. Gran is making sympathetic noises.

Then she says, 'Well we knew he didn't have long. Dave had already recorded his bark.'

I realise they're talking about a dead dog. I want to laugh though it is quite sad.

'Lets go down by the water.' I follow Failand.

'Dont go far you two.' We say we're going to use the toilet in the Llandoger Trow.

'The Llandoger Trow was a Welsh boat, that went up the Severn,' says Grandad.

'Quick before he starts on about building the bridges.' I say to Failand. We giggle like we're escaping on a boat up the Severn ourselves.

Down by the river we lean on the rails and the swans are white blobs on the dark water especially the ones with their heads folded up. There's a bridge with arches lit up, like a bridge in a postcard. I want to send it to someone but I don't know who.

'It looks like the Seine,' says Failand who is still thinking about Paris. She says she'll be going soon. The people here are all younger. A couple of boys come up from another Pub. There's a lot of Pubs. There's even a boat Pub or floating restaurant as it calls itself.

'Hi girls, you off the boat?' says one of them and I think he means have you just arrived as though we'd come from another country and were a bit green but it turns out he thinks we live on a boat. There's a boat with a cat flap and a grey and white cat comes out. A ship's cat? Mum bought a ships cat, not a real one but one made of cats fur to give to my Auntie Jo, well it was supposed to be a replica of a ships cat that had been to the Antartic or somewhere with a Captain Shackleton who I hadn't heard of.

I want to say, 'Is this a replica cat?' but I don't' as I don't think they'd know about Shackleton's cat or my Auntie Jo's birthday.

'We've come for the jazz,' I say instead and the other one laughs as though I'm joking.

'Her Grandad plays, she's come to support him,' says Failand which makes it sound OK, to be here with your grandparents like you're doing them a favour and he could almost be playing. He did once though I'm not sure what.

'What does he play?' asks the taller one as if he's trying to catch us out.

'Guitar,' I say as everyone played the guitar then.

'Clarinet,' says Failand at the same time but they don't seem to notice. I expect they think he plays both or aren't interested in Jazz anyway. One of them puts his arm round me. I feel half pleased and half embarrassed. Will Failand think I'm used to letting boys I don't know put their arms round me? I can't push him away as that would be making it seem like a big deal. Like I thought I was being sexually assaulted when he was just being friendly. Do they realise how young we are? Some girls of twelve look quite old I know. We don't.

Do they care? I mean lots of young girls are prostitutes in some countries, like Thailand and get married at our age in India or Africa and girls in this country are always having babies while they're still at school. We're only talking. Not getting pregnant or taking drugs or being trafficked.

'You got a boyfriend?' says the other one, the tall one to Failand.

'Yes, Billy.'

'Where's Billy tonight?'

'In his stable.'

I can tell he doesn't like it. And I think she's trying to make him look stupid. He's got sticky up dark hair and a short sleeved white shirt and is quite good looking.

'What's your name?' says mine. I don't mean he's mine, just the one with his arm round me.

'Mattie,'

'Mattie?' he says sort of surprised. And I think he thinks it's a show off kind of name. Once I said to Mum why did you call me after a book by Roald Dahl and she said she didn't she called me after a name she saw it on a gravestone when she was pregnant and trying to think of a name. My other Gran, Mum's mother, asked her why she was calling me Matilda and Mum said she thought it was a perfectly good name. Nan said, 'For a gravestone perhaps but not a new baby.' I think this boy thinks its an old fashioned name too but I can't change it now.

'We've got a cat called Mattie,' is all he says.

'I bet you havn't got a cat called Failand,' says Failand to the other one.

'I've got a dog called Ace. He's a card,' he says and laughs at his own joke which I think he may have made before.

'What's yours?' I'm interested in names.

'Danny,' which is pretty common, but OK. The other one says his name is Lee which sounds like someone being done for driving without a licence. I wonder if they have a car.

'Wanna a drink Mattie?' says Danny as though we've known each other for ages.

'Where?' says Failand sounding up for it.

'In the Bed,' he says and I pull away. Then I see the Pub opposite, a pretty Pub lit up with red and blue lighting next door to the Llandoger is called The Bed. I think it's a stupid name for a Pub. It looks old underneath the lights. But Danny says it's a new Pub. We walk by The Bed which has its name reflected in lights on the pavement.

'You're in bed now girls,' says Lee. The Bed is now written on us instead of on the pavement. I think how versatile light is, like in a camera, how it can make images. Perhaps it can make Christopher appear. Maybe the Llandoger isn't old either just a copy or a replica like Mr. Chips, who was Captain Shackleton's cat who went to the Antarctic.

I say this about the pub not the cat and Danny says, 'No it is old, my Grandad used to go there.'

'Mine still does,' I say and they laugh and feel like old friends. Then Gran calls out.

'D'you want these cokes you two, they're losing their fizz?' and I suppose she's trying to get us back without sounding like she's worried about us or does she think its alright. I'm quite glad of an excuse to get away but I also feel I shouldn't want to, like going on Safari and being afraid when you see a lion. Once when we had to say what we'd like to be when we grew up I said, 'A Wildlife photographer' everyone laughed as though I wasn't wildlife photographer material. The thing is I quite like standing by a river with a boy with his arm round me. But I'm a bit worried about it too.

'Your eyes are very blue,' Danny says then, which they are, even Sophe says so. I mean he's noticed it himself not just saying it. I don't know what to say to him. Suddenly there's a loud splash and lots of lights. Someone's fallen into the river or even jumped off the bridge. I shudder and Danny tightens his arm round me and I feel scared but excited. There's an ambulance on the bridge and someone else jumps into the river. Then Lee laughs.

'It's not funny,' I say and I'm really worried someone's drowned.

'It is, it's a film, they're filming Casualty.' Then I can see the film crew on the bridge and I'm relieved but I felt cheated. I mean though I was glad no one was getting drowned it felt like another trick, like nothing was real.

'Sorry boys we've got to go. Her Grandad's playing and its his birthday, we promised to listen.' Failand lies again but I'm glad she can handle it. I don't think Failand will ever be a schoolgirl mother.

'They're just kids,' I hear Lee say as we walk off. It doesn't matter. I feel quite grown up actually and we laugh all the way home as though we were drunk. Gran and Grandad don't say anything, well not till we come back past Ashton Court and there's lights and music and people walking along the pavement like it really was a medieval fair.

'What's happening now?'

'Its the glow,' they say all together again which sounds like a strange local custom handed down over the ages.

'The Glow?' I realise it must be something to do with the balloons but I don't think the balloons would go up at night. They usually go up in the morning or evening.

'They glow to music,' explains Failand as though it was a dance.

'They turn on the fires and light them up but its such a crowd and no where to park. I forgot it was tonight,' says Gran. I didn't think it was something you could forget.

'We can go on Saturday and see the ascent,' says Grandad, another word that sounds as if its part of a ritual. I was sorry about not seeing the glow but it was nice seeing all the people walking home and going back to their camper vans and the little church tower floodlit like it was religion against witchcraft.

When I go to bed Christopher is there and he looks very young, a boy playing with his toys. There was this picture once in an encyclopaedia of an aristocratic family. It said about how one of them died when she was ten. A little girl with flowers in her hair playing with a kitten. I thought how she didn't know that when she was being painted with her brothers and sisters. I wondered if she died before the kitten. Well they're all dead now.

'You Ok?' I say in a big sisterly kind of way. I feel the night has made me older. He shrugs. He's drawing something childish on a piece of paper, an animal, a simple kind of animal.

'I want to be a caveman,' he says seriously.

I laugh then and remember saying I wanted to be a wildlife photographer and people laughing at me. And Sophe saying I had more chance of being a ballet dancer which isn't true. Its easier to photograph a herd of elephants than be a ballet dancer. The animal does look like animals on cave walls and Christopher looks absorbed. I think of Jasmine's brother at the Zoo who looked so absorbed by the animals. I suppose the cave people who drew pictures on cave walls were the first artists. Did they think it was important or more like graffiti. Did someone say, 'Go out and catch a bison, don't just draw it.' Perhaps Christopher means he wants to be an archaeologist like on Timewatch. I feel sad for him because he isn't going to grow up. When children get murdered it says in the paper what they wanted to be, a model or a footballer. I wonder what people would say if I got murdered. Would they say she wanted to be a wildlife photographer as though that was my ambition not just an idea.

What if Christopher had been murdered and that's why no one will talk about it. I think I'd have heard if someone in my family had been murdered. Then Christopher disappeared again and I don't blame him. I go to bed. I'm used to having a ghost around even if I can't handle real boys. Some people would be seriously scared. I dream I'm in a cave and Danny comes to rescue me. Ed is there too but he turns into Miles and starts laughing at us as though we've done something stupid and Sophe is there and says, 'You want to be careful going into caves with strangers, you could get into serious trouble.' And then she jumps over a bridge and it isn't a television serial but she's really drowned And a band is playing at her funeral, a marching band.

I've woken up feeling really scared and my legs feel all funny as though I know its only a dream and Marley is asleep on my bed curled up like Shackleton's cat but flicking its tail to show its alive.

CHAPTER THIRTEEN

I don't see Failand the next day. Me and Gran go to the supermarket and Grandad has to pick us up to take the shopping home. Gran says she's shattered. He says we can eat out somewhere as having me staying with them is like their holiday too. Its as if I'm a destination to be explored. Gran perks up and so do I. We go to a place called Portishead which isn't very far away and was a Port I suppose. Its not got much sea and no beach except some shingle, but mostly beach grass and a headland. There is a lake with boats on. Gran of course remembers taking out rowing boats, when she came here with her school friends Diane and Elizabeth, on their bikes. I never thought of Gran having school friends only her sister and Christopher. Whats more interesting than the rowing boats are some sailing boats. They're not so much toy boats as model boats, really nice boats and it isn't children playing with them but old men. They're remote controlled and the men are standing by the side of the lake holding control panels. Except for one sitting all by himself under a tree with silver leaves and staring out on this lake as though it was real lake. Like in Canada somewhere and it was real boats. I wonder if Grandad wishes he had one. One of the model ones I mean.

'Who does he think he is, Captain Ahab? Thar she blows,' he says sarcastically so perhaps he doesn't. I know who would, Christopher. If he'd lived he'd be here today clutching his remote. I pick out a boat for him, one with dark red sails. I even think I'll tell him about it tonight as if he was a real person. Perhaps I'm cracking up.

There's a Muscovy duck a little boy is trying to feed but it walks away rather awkwardly as though its very old and very cross. But maybe its just how Muscovy ducks look all the time.

'I know how it feels,' says Gran. She's sat on a seat sagging somehow like a puppet without its strings. 'Whoever said Ugly Ducklings,' she says as a family of swans go by, two white parents with orange beaks and six grey cygnets all looking proud as swans do.

'Hans Christian Andersen,' says Grandad.

'I was being rhetorical,' says Gran.

'Lets go find our lunch,' says Grandad as though we were going to catch it in the lake. It seems we have to walk to a chosen Pub that does food and Gran's not too pleased with the idea. Then they have this argument they've had before about who's going to die first like its an old people's game. Also its as if dying first was winning when its losing. Like what you're going to be when you grow up is a young persons game but you might choose the crappiest job even though you wouldn't want to do it really. We decide to walk and Grandad says he'll show me a garden with a dragon in it as if I was about five. Then there really is a garden with a dragon in it. A life size dragon, well I don't know what size a dragon is as there's no such thing but this one looks about the right size for a dragon if there was. Ed would understand. Anyway its pretty big as garden ornaments go and the houses along here are all big with lots of chimneys and looking out to sea. The sea is grey and not really a sea but an estuary and the road is dark on account of a wood up above on the other side so its not as good as it sounds. A man comes by on a black horse and you could almost imagine he's out of a Victorian murder mystery.

There's a little platform at the end to look out to sea and a view of two bridges. The bridges are both Severn bridges so I s'pose that makes it the Severn which is a river. I told you it wasn't a sea.

'Did Isambard make them?' I ask. Gran says it was after his time and they both remember both bridges being built but not both at once. The first one was built when my

Dad was born. Before that there was a ferry, and Gran had gone over on it when she was a girl.

'On a dark and stormy night,' I say.

'It was raining,' says Gran, 'I felt like I was on the Bayeaux tapestry.'

Grandad says it wasn't raining on the Bayeaux tapestry. They'd seen it in Normandy. The original that was made in 1066 when the Normans landed and Harold got shot in the eye with an arrow. Then he said what he'd noticed most was how awkward the horses looked on those little needlework boats.

It's really hot today and the Pub has a big garden full of people eating and a white marquee as if there's a wedding though there isn't. Gran thinks its too hot to sit outside, she looks hot, her face is all flushed. I want to be outside and see the two bridges and a big ship going by. Well not so much a ship as a container. It's quite a big Pub. It used to be a hotel where people stopped before going on a voyage though it's hardly the Atlantic ocean though maybe it leads out to sea like rivers do on maps. What I notice is a picture of old Portishead on the wall with these girls with bikes, lined up by the lake wearing really old fashioned clothes.

'Oh look you and Diane and Elizabeth on your bike ride,' I say to Gran.

'I don't think those girls ever crossed either of the Severn Bridges, ' Grandad is picking out his onion rings. 'Why do Pubs love onion rings,' he asks.

'I think they invented them,' Gran agrees. 'I don't think I can eat this, I'm sorry,' she pushes aside her steak sounding sad as if it was a tragedy. I think old people hate to waste things because of the war, even if they can't remember the war they can remember rationing. I'm also thinking that though the girls in the picture with their bikes were before Gran's time they were doing the same thing and children are doing the same thing today only the bikes and the clothes have changed. When we get home Gran opens her handbag and unwraps her piece of steak, its in a red paper serviette from the Pub. She offers it to Marley who isn't very keen. I cut it up into little pieces as I know what Spider likes and I know Gran feels bad about wasting the steak. Marley shows a bit more enthusiasm and Gran looks happier.

'Have you taken your tablets?' asks Grandad, 'You haven't run out have you?'

'Don't keep on,' says Gran a bit embarrassed and turns to me and says.

'Everyone takes tablets if they're over sixty,' she says.

'I don't.' says Granda all pleased with himself.

'My Dad does,' I say which is true and think of all the tablets Ed takes but don't say about them.

'Oh we're all going to live forever,' says Grandad, 'for what its worth.' I think it would be worth a lot, everlasting life. I think I might be a chemist when I grow up. Also I feel better about Ed, not that he'll live forever but that they can make him better.

The next day is the balloon festival and I ask if we're going. I want to go as it seems important with all the posters and it's even on television. Gran and Grandad don't seem so keen. But we actually do go in the end. It's still hot.

'Its going to be crowded,' says Gran which it is. There's loads of people and cars all blocking the roads. It doesn't look like where we went riding. Its bigger than Scarborough Fair. There is a fair there and rides and tents with things in. I buy a cat cushion to take home for Spider because it's got a black and white cat on that looks like her. I buy a handmade birdhouse for mum though we've already got one but no birds have ever nested in it. I'm trying to find something for Ed.

'Christopher, my brother bought a water pistol here once,' says Gran.

'But Christopher's younger than Ed.' I say as if Christopher's still here. Its like we're talking about last year not half a century ago.

'And they're weren't so many stalls or things,' says Gran, 'we weren't spoilt for choice.'

'We weren't spoilt for anything, we made our own fun out of used matchsticks,' says Grandad. I suppose he is joking though I think of him glued to Blue Peter with a box of burnt out matches making a suspension bridge.

'Did they have Blue Peter then?' I ask.

'We didn't even have television, well not in our house,' says Gran, then more worriedly, 'we didn't have the balloon festival either.'

'The phantom water pistol,' says Grandad. I try to remember if I've ever seen Christopher with a water pistol. I havn't.

'It must have been at the Agricultural Show,' says Gran, 'we always had that, the grounds were private then and you only came here for the Show. It all belonged Lady Smythe who was still alive then, I never saw her but I knew people who did. She was quite famous. It belongs to Bristol now.

'I think all Bristol's turned up,' says Grandad. There are a lot of people considering its just balloons going up and they go up any day. 'Now the balloons are entering the arena.' says the man on the microphone like it was a bullfight. Its just a fenced off patch of grass. The balloons are towed in by four wheel drives. Each balloon has its own trailer like a horsebox but smaller. Its quite boring actually if you're not going up in one. The man on the microphone tries to make it sound exciting as the balloons are laid out flat on the grass like maps. As they get blown up they turn into globes.

'Hardly, Around the World in Eighty Days,' says Gran which is an old film I may have seen on telly. I think of these balloons going round the world it makes it feel more exciting. Watching the burners shooting fire up is good and all the people sat on the grass and the girls coming by in short skirts and children running about.

'What happens if it rains do they still go up?' I ask. Grandad's gone to find a beer tent.

'Rain,' says Gran really sarcastically and I think she's going to say it'd take more than a drop of rain to stop the balloon festival. Instead she says a gnat flying the wrong way could stop it. I can see what she means. Even when the balloons are inflated none seem to be taking off. It's the wind apparently, its the wrong kind of wind.

The balloons are all advertising something or somewhere. One is shaped like a can of beer, there's even a house. I like the traditional ones best. There's one advertising champagne which actually manages to take off and the announcer gets really excited. I'm almost getting excited myself. There's a Rupert Bear one, I mean it is Rupert Bear himself, well a balloon Rupert and he's having trouble getting up.

'Come on children, give Rupert a big cheer,' begs the announcer and the children cheer and Rupert's big balloon hand waves out then goes down again.

By now there are about three balloon's in the sky and moving off really fast as balloons do.

'Where are they going?' I ask.

'Not very far,' says Gran.

'That's why they had to go on and invent the aeroplane,' says Grandad who's come back from the beer tent complaining about queues and plastic glasses.

129

'I think its the journey not the arrival,' says Gran. 'Something the Owl and Pussy Cat might have gone on, on their honeymoon in.' She adds and I can see what she means. There's quite a few up there by now, a mass ascent, the man on the mike calls it but I wouldn't go that far.

'They look good,' I say, which is true I think of them going over Isambard's suspension bridge like on the postcards.

'They look better from the garden,' says Gran but I think its better here with the hot air burners close up breathing dragon fire and all the people watching. I wish Sophe was here. It would be her kind of thing, not actually watching but making fun of the balloon man. Not the balloons themselves. A big striped one has got snagged in some trees and others are coming down still in Ashton Court. Grandad is laughing. I'm feeling sorry for the announcer.

'They need remote controls,' I say thinking of the model boats on Portishead lake.

'I don't think that's the object of the exercise,' says Grandad.

'Its more like going camping,' says Gran. I don't know if she means the flames or having to rely on the weather.

'Back to nature,' Grandad agrees.

Gran says its too hot and she'll go and sit in the rose garden. I think she's joking like she was pretending to be the lady of the manor but there really is a rose garden apparently.

'Is your mobile charged?' Grandad sounds bossy but Gran is always forgetting things, usually her glasses.

Grandad says he'll take me on the rides. I'm not sure I want to go on the rides but Grandad's keen. I like the fair part and Grandad's getting jolly, probably the effect of the beer tent.

'Give the lady a coconut,' he shouts, there aren't any coconuts only giant soft toys, a dog or a leopard, you see people who've won one wearing it round their necks like extra children. I agree to go on the dodgems and Grandad is taking it seriously and bumping into as many people as he can. He's the oldest person on the dodgems. Everyone's laughing or screaming and I begin to enjoy it too but I'm glad when they stop. When we get off Grandad says he's got to find the toilets.

'Never be an old man Mattie,' he says. Which isn't likely but I don't s'pose its any worse than being an old woman. You can't really miss the toilets they're in blue boxes like you might expect to see a guardsman at Buckingham Palace and there is a queue.

'Where's your mate?' calls a boy who I don't recognise at first then I see he's with his mate, its the boys from the Jazz Pub night.

'She's gone to the toilet,' I say as I don't want to look as if I'm with my Grandad again. They laugh.

'We saw you on the dodgems with your Grandad,' says Dan.

'It must be his birthday again,' says Lee.

'Want to come on the dodgems with me Mattie?' he's remembered my name and I'm quite pleased at first then I think its because its the same as his cat.

'Yes it's Dan's birthday,' says Lee. I feel embarrassed and want to get away, I can't handle them on my own and I'm afraid Grandad will appear and claim me. Anyway I don't know if they're serious. Two girls are going past them to get on the dodgems, they've got short denim skirts and long brown legs.

'Want to share a car girls?' asks Lee.

'Who's paying?' the girls start giggling as they divide themselves up between two cars with their long legs all over the place like giraffes. I don't think I'll ever have long legs. I might giggle at boys but not today. Actually I'm glad I'm let off, but I'm also annoyed they've forgotten me already. I'm not sure where Grandad is. I don't know if he's still in one of the toilets, looking for me, or gone to the Rose Garden.

I feel in my pocket for my mobile. It isn't charged. Its going to be the Zoo all over again. Some children with painted faces go by and I almost expect to see Jasmine. I step on someone's picnic rug and a dog snarls at me as if the rug had become his garden. There's so many people I must make a plan. Ed always says its best to have a plan even if you don't use it. I don't believe in having a plan till you need one. My plan is to find the rose garden and then I can phone Grandad from Gran's mobile. There aren't any signposts. I go past the fair to where we went on the horses. I wish I had a horse. There's the big house which is Ashton Court which I go right round, its yellow on one side like a Pub and round the back what Failand said used to be stables and even her Dad can remember horses there who used to pull the Lord Mayors coach. I think there's still horse in Ashton Court but not today. The house is so long at the front with a big lawn where we saw the bridesmaids. I go down some steps and I come to some little graves. Like toy graves. Then I think perhaps the children of the house had private burials as it was probably Victorian times and they all died of TB. It says, Sylvie on one who only lived for about ten years back when Gran and Grandad would just be born. Some were before that. Then it said. 'Little Chloe of Otter, and Kim faithful companion for seventeen years.' I realise its all dead dogs. A canine graveyard.

'I wonder where they buried the horses?' says a man to his wife. Their little boy has a bucket and spade and looks like he's trying to dig up the dog's bones as though he was a dog himself. There's a picture of a crab on the bucket, perhaps they'd meant to go to the seaside and got diverted. I go up some steps and there's a pond with a live dog in it. I wonder if faithful Kim ever played in this pond. A woman's taking a photo of the dog. I don't suppose Kim had his photo taken but I don't suppose the dog in the pond will have his own gravestone. A squirrel is sat by the pond as though squirrels ate fish, he's eating something. Then he turns and runs up a tree, a huge tree with an enormous trunk. It must be like living in the big house to a squirrel.

I walk to the edge of the lawn and look down and there is the rose garden and there's Gran sitting on a bench and I can smell the roses though they're going over.

'You look like you live here,' I say despite the fairground behind her and one of the scarier looking rides is clawing the sky like a monster crustacean.

'A live-in maid perhaps,' she says, then, 'I wonder there they put the washing line?' as though she really was imagining hanging out the clothes and a blackbird about to peck off her nose.

'I don't know, where Grandad is?'

'I do, he's rung, he's on his way.' Grandad is coming, a bit unsteadily I think he's come via the beer tent. He stops to pick a rose and put it in his buttonhole.

'Ready ladies?' We go back through the tents and I buy a black T shirt for Ed with Bristol Balloons written on it and a clump of balloon's going up in the air. It seems important to have it now but I know it won't mean much to Ed. You have to be at the balloon festival to understand it. I don't even know if he'll wear it? We leave in a crowd of people and baby buggies and dogs and up above a sky full of balloons floating over us towards Bristol. We go out through a house built into the wall which must have been where people lived who guarded the gates. A Gatehouse I suppose which I've heard of but never noticed before though I have been round castles. Gran says my Dad went to a birthday party there when he was a little boy and Harvey, the birthday boy, had a cake shaped like a train but nobody else came because it was the summer holidays and they'd all forgotten. I can almost see the cake train as if it was still in the window.

I watch people cross the road and slip under the wire to their mobile homes. There are crowds at the bus stops on both sides of the road. On our side they wait beneath a copper beech while the others go off to their cars which are parked in the fields round about. Grandad has parked up a side street as the fields charge £5 a car.

'Better rates than grazing,' says Grandad.

'But a shorter season than strawberries,' gasps Gran. She's out of breath walking to the car.

'Maybe Grandad will have to pay to park inside the walls next year,' I say.

'We may not go next year,' says Gran as if she's had enough, 'unless you're here again,' she adds.

'Our catalyst,' says Grandad and I like to think I'm a catalyst. Someone who makes things happen just by being here. A pink balloon drifts across the road as though it was as tired as Gran and then lifts up again on a new burst of fire. But its struggling like an oily seabird.

CHAPTER FOURTEEN

On Sunday some people come over to play cards. I am included but reluctantly, they want to play serious cards. I spend quite a lot of time on the phone talking to Mum and home comes back to me gradually I was afraid I was losing it. Now I feel homesick and worried about Ed and feel like they're floating away like ducks when you run out of bread.

The next day Gran says we can go to Weston on the bus and sit upstairs and look down on all the fields and gardens drying up in the hot weather. She makes it sound like the journey is the thing, not Weston. Then Failand rings and says do I want to go out with her and her Mum and Ham. They're going on a picnic to Weston. I do but I think of Gran having asked first. I say to Gran about the alternative Weston trip.

'That'll be nice, I'll see if my hairdresser can fit me in and I can go to my painting class with Linda. She's been emailing me.' Gran sounds more pleased than sorry, almost as if she's been trying to get rid of me.

I've never met Linda but I think of her as looking like Miss Marples and the dead dog who lost its lead. I feel Grans wants a break from me more than I want a break from her. I'd never thought I could be in the way or that I was stopping her doing her own thing. Now I can see she must have been doing other things before I came and I was interrupting her from her friends like I was interrupted from Sophe.

'Sorry,' I say, 'I never thought.'

'Never mind its good practice for being a teenager,' says Gran as though I really was being selfish. Which I didn't think was fair. I didn't ask to come here. She asked me.

"I'll look all glamorous when you get back,' it seems her hairdresser can fit her in.

Nina's got a big car, almost a people carrier, Hamish is already in the front. Me and Failand get in and spread ourselves about. At the last minute Miles and John, who've been practising their guitar playing, in a sort of conservatory, run up and say they're coming.

'How's your brother?' Nina asks in a really nice way.

'I think he's OK, he's had his treatment, but he had a friend in hospital who died and it upset him.'

I think the others are a bit awed by the seriousness and I almost don't want to talk about Ed because it makes him sound like a sick person instead of Ed himself who's more like Miles than Ham. I don't mean Ham is ill only that he's someone you might ask how he is. He's quiet in the car till we're overtaken by some noisy motorbikes and Miles says how fast they are.

'Five of them,' says Ham and sounds like one of the boys and I'm glad for him. Then they keep asking him how many this or that and spoil it. Like how many sheep or cows in a field which you couldn't count anyway, which confuses him. Three men cross the road with guns and dogs.

'Nine,' say Ham without being asked.

'Nine, how does that add up?' asks John.

'Three dogs, three men, three guns.' Ham keeps on saying numbers but you're not quite sure what he's counting. It could be trees or cars or signposts or houses. Or he could be adding them all together.

'Life's just one big sum to Ham,' says Nina but she doesn't sound upset like Gran said. I mean about Ham being different but I suppose she's got used to it. I suppose you can adjust to anything. Gran had to adjust to her brother dying. I don't want to have to adjust to my brother dying.

'What d'you want to be when you grow up? Asks Failand.

'I don't know,' I say feeling pathetic. I don't want to mention the wildlife photographer again or a film director because its sounds as bad as saying a celebrity and as unlikely. Failand says she liked to be a pilot but she'll probably end up a teacher of some sort.

'I want to be a banker, its where the money is,' says John. Then he says about his parents coming here from Nigeria to go to University and then staying on after he was born. He says his older brother stayed in Nigeria with his grandmother because he'd been born there. He said he might go and join him when he had a degree or he might become a Londoner. He made London sound like a different country. I've only been to London once, we went on a tour bus and Miles said it was like a tour round the News.

'Where are we going today?' asks Miles sounding impatient. I don't think he knows what he wants to be when he grew up either.

'Weston.'

'Weston, why Weston?'

'There's nothing at Weston,' John agrees.

'There's the pier and the amusements, fish and chips and the sand and the sea,' says Nina.

'And Donkeys,' says Ham.

137

'And the roads, don't forget the roads,' says Miles which I think is a joke from a film. Something I've heard Ed say.

'We go to Weston more often than the sea does,' says Failand which I don't get. Then John explains the tide's never in at Weston. He calls me Mat which sounds friendly and I think we've got over the colour clash.

Just when I'm thinking how good Weston sounds we see a sign for Cheddar.

'Lets go to Cheddar.' Miles says.

'Yeah I want to be a caveman.' John says in a singy way. I nearly say that's what Christopher said then I remember he's only a ghost. Well not only a ghost as a ghost is rarer than a person even if it isn't so substantial. I wanted to go to Weston and see if the tide was in and maybe go on the dodgems with Miles. Failand could go on with John. I didn't say any of this as it wasn't my car. Nina took the Cheddar road. I didn't mind that much and if we had gone on the dodgems I suppose Miles and John would have gone in one car and me and Failand in another. I don't even like dodgems, it sounds like somewhere Gran might have met boys when she was a girl.

We park at the bottom by the town which has a little stone place that looks very old like where they sold the first piece of cheddar cheese. A boy and girl are sat there now passing each other a can of something, cider probably. I think of telling Sophe I'm in cider country. But I'll do it tonight when I get back. We go over a little bridge with a long tailed bird in the water hopping about on the stones.

'A grey wagtail,' says Miles but it looks quite yellow to me.

You don't get the effect of caves and cavemen or even a gorge at first because there are so many little shops selling cheese and pixies. There was a talking sheep dog, well a model of a dog. It was telling you to come and see them making cheese. Ham was really into it. He was telling it to bark. I thought he might think it was a real dog talking, not because he was thick so much as not being surprised by anything.

'I want to listen to the talking dog,' he says when Failand pulls him away but as if he knows it isn't a real dog. I think he was just going along with it.

'Come on Ham you can't stand there all day talking to a battery operated canine. We're so going to have to disown you,' says Miles.

'D'you want to go to the caves and see a skeleton?' John asks. I think that's what he wants to do. John I mean.

'I loathe skeletons.' Ham says in a posh voice as though he's taking someone off but I don't think he is.

'There might be a talking one, I wouldn't put it past them, its so tacky.' Failand says. When we get round the corner there's a pond or a small lake you could see fish in and I remembered the fish in the garden when I was with Miles and I wondered if he did? We stopped in this Pub garden and drank coke and watched the waterfall or weir as Miles called it. There were little cottages on the hill and you could imagine people living in them and growing cabbages and runner beans like old Charlie, and picking strawberries in summer. This is a strawberry place but it isn't strawberry time. They have cheese all the year round. Like we can get anything in the supermarket because its imported but they would only get strawberries in strawberry time. There's a sweet shop making its own sweets and then a surprising thing, a toy museum. Its got dinky toys in the window, cars and tractors but I can't find ours. I mean mine and Christopher's. The ones we race with. I sort of imagine him here with his nose pressed to the glass like something out of Dickens. There's a notice saying they buy old toy cars and I think of Gran or Grandad bringing Christopher's cars here to sell and him not being able to find them. I'm glad they don't like coming to Cheddar.

'It must have been boring being young in the fifties, glad I wasn't born before computer games,' says Miles but John looks quite interested. I wonder if Christopher came here. But it wouldn't be a museum then, just a shop and the toys would be new. Ham disappears into another shop selling dragons and glass flowers. He's watching a glass blower blowing glass under a flame. The glass is gone soft in the heat.

'Looks like Hannibal Lector,' says Miles and the man doing it does look a bit like a wax figure or someone who might do something drastic. I wish Ed was here, it's the sort of thing he likes.

We get to the caves at last and there's a very old skeleton. They'd found someone alive living in Cheddar who was related to him by his DNA sais Nina which seems spooky. Like you could dig someone up out of a graveyard who's been dead for hundreds of years and still be able to get his DNA and match him up with someone alive now. It didn't make being a ghost so amazing. Well amazing enough but not so amazing. That there was something left so you'd know it was your great, great, well however many greats it would take, without him having a gravestone with a name on. I try to say this but it doesn't come out right.

'What if they exhumed one of your ancestors and you found you weren't the Lord of the Manor after all. Your great grandmother might have been having it off with the gamekeeper,' Miles seems pleased with this story.

'The dead didn't used to tell tales,' says Nina.

'They did, they wrote books,' says Failand.

'Like Dickens,' I say.

'If you like, I meant ghost writers,' she says. I have heard of ghost writers, writers who write memoirs for celebrities who cant be bothered to write themselves. But I like reading old books better. That's what I'd found with Chloe, we both liked reading the same books and talking about them. I think I might make friends with her when I get back.

'I expect they have a lot of rows in heaven,' says John. I thought of ghosts fighting each other which would be a bit like balloons fighting. I mean proper ghosts in white sheets.

'I used to know a girl who's family came from Cheddar, who said she saw a skeleton in her Gran's house,' says Failand. I wanted to say I'd met a ghost in my Gran's bedroom but I didn't as it would sound like I'd made it up or a joke. Which would be unfair to Christopher because he'd trusted me enough to appear.

'What was she on?' says John and I was glad I hadn't.

We went in the caves, well all except Nina and Ham. The caves weren't as scary as the skeleton having relatives but different. Like a foreign country is different when you get off the plane and feel the warmth in the air. Here you felt the chill. We had a guide and the rocks all had names and stories. He said they might have had human sacrifices which didn't seem so surprising when you're underground.

'Who'd find the evidence?' asked Failand as though she'd killed someone herself.

'It would be in a glass case by now,' says Miles.

'Much too late I'd have calcified by then,' she says as though she'd really got away with murder though it wouldn't be murder if everyone was doing it. Just ritual. There were dripping rocks that looked like frozen waterfalls and maybe they were once, but you can't turn into stone overnight, not like water into ice. I think of the brittle glass melted and being reshaped with just a flame and how it would stay a glass daffodil. Well till it broke. I'm trying to work this out, how it's too big to get your head round like climate change.

'Amazing,' says Miles. 'Think of the timespan.'

'Nothings forever,' says Failand and I wish I'd said that till John says, 'but some are for longer than others,' which sounded better than what I was trying to say.

There were stalagtites and stalagmites which have taken nearly forever to form but all stones are old. When we were in Mr. Allan's class, he was telling us about evolution and how long it took for fish to grow wings how we couldn't comprehend the timescale even though there was a diagram. Nathan put his hand up, 'How come a caterpillar can turn into a butterfly and a tadpole and grow legs in a couple of months then sir?' which rather threw Mr. Allan.

I nearly fell over in the cave and gave a little cry. I told you I was a wimp. But there was a feeling if you fell over in the cave you'd never get up again and never get out. Miles put out his hand to help me, I didn't take it, but I wanted to.

I was glad to come out but I still felt the caveness about me like the sun's come out but your coats still wet. We walked up through the gorge which was pretty impressive when you looked up. Miles said it was more like the wild west and a cowboy would just jump over it.

'Champion the Wonder horse,' says John jumping up in the air like a little boy. The posters say it was formed by melt water. I'm not sure what kind of water that is. Well if it was melt water it must have melted, so it must have been ice. I suppose when the ice age melted it all ran down here in a great rush parting the rocks like in the bible when the red sea got separated for Moses to let his people through.

I say it was hard to imagine water gushing down to make the gorge millions of years ago but Failand says it wasn't that hard and there'd been a flood not very long ago, well not long in Cheddar time. It had been on television and all the water had come gushing down then which was a bit like the caterpillar turning into a butterfly when it had taken the fish ages to turn into a bird.

We sat on the rocks and ate the food and looked like a big family.

'All we need is Timmy the dog,' Miles said.

'Then we could have a proper adventure,' said Failand in a child reading voice.

'I wish I was a dog,' said Ham. I suppose it was a family joke, something to do with the Famous Five books by Enid Blyton. I haven't read them but I know about them so I must have read about them somewhere. John didn't look as though he was in on it either. The five included Timmy the dog which made Enid Blyton sound like Ham. And it made me and John like the odd ones out as if we were the town cousins who didn't know how to row a boat or ride a horse or where the treasure was hidden.

There were signs saying, Beware of Falling Rocks.

'If we don't get attacked by the beast of the Mendips we get buried under rockfall, this is dangerous territory,' says Miles.

'Dangerous? Man you 'aint ever been to my country,' says John.

'Nor have you,' says Miles and they start fighting but not very seriously.

'Oh I don't know, like Clifton is pretty scary on a Saturday night,' says Failand sarcastically.

'Well we've got our own gorge,' says John and I remember going to the Zoo and over the bridge.

'Is Ham with you?' calls Nina who was sitting on a stone a bit further away packing up the picnic things. He wasn't.

'Oh not another Ham search,' says Miles as though this happened all the time. Then he offered to go back down to the caves to see if he was there.

'Ham is like a ghost,' Failand says and I feel my stomach turn over as though he was dead. Then she says, 'Always disappearing.'

We went to the Amusements which is where they usually find him apparently and we went to the shop with the glassblower but he wasn't there either. John and Miles said they'd stay in the Amusements as he might turn up. Nina went to get the car and we drove up and parked by the falling rock notices and walked on up the gorge. We had to keep ringing each other to say we hadn't found him

'If only Ham had a mobile,' I said to Failand.

'He has.'

'Does he know how to use it?'

'Of course.' says Failand unhelpfully

'But he doesn't know when', says Nina wearily.

'He doesn't consider himself lost,' says Failand.

'Well in a way he isn't,' Nina seemed half worried and half resigned. It seems this happens quite often. There weren't many people that high up, just two women painting with easels like they were in a painting themselves. I think of Gran and Linda at their painting class. I'll tell her about the women when I get back. I wonder if she ever comes here to paint? I've forgotten she doesn't like coming to Cheddar, she doesn't even know I'm here.

Nina asks them if they've seen Ham but they haven't. Their paintings are of rocks and look quite good. I see a boy who I think I know and I go to shout out then I realise its Christopher. Anyway he doesn't turn round when I all out which kind of embarrasses Failand.

'You don't have to involve the whole gorge.' She says and I realize she can't see Christopher and msut be wondering what I'm shouting about.

'Sorry, I say, ' thought I saw someone I knew,'

There's no one there, she says lets go down don't worry he'll turn up,' as if he was my brother not hers.

I didn't recognise him because it wasn't a place I'd expect to see him. When you see people in places you don't expect them to be, you don't recognise them at first. Well I don't. Ed says it's a girl thing. Once on holiday in Cornwall I saw Eva who goes to my school, in a café in St. Ives. I didn't recognise her but she spoke to me as though we were big friends though we didn't speak to each other at school. She really seemed like my friend and we went on the beach together and watched fish being unloaded from a boat and a man was sat on a seat reading the paper and a seagull came down and grabbed his pasty. He looked really cross and threw a pebble at another seagull who was sat on an upturned boat.

'The seagull is innocent,' shouted Eva which seemed very funny at the time, we were only ten, we kept laughing for ages. When we got back to school we went back to not speaking to each other.

The other thing I feel is, afraid. I've never felt afraid of Christopher not even the first time I saw him. I don't feel afraid of him now. I feel afraid for him. Like someone in a film who's going into the cellar to escape the murderer and you know it's the very worst place they could go.

Then I thought Ham might have fallen down a cave but I didn't say so.

'As long as he hasn't fallen down a cave,' says Failand like she's reading my mind, I hope not. I hope nobody finds out how to read minds while I'm alive. Though I'm not thinking anything bad, well only what she's thinking. I suppose its quite an obvious thing to say in Cheddar like you'd say you hoped someone hadn't drowned if you'd lost them by the sea. Nina looks worried but says they'd hear him if he had.

'He wouldn't go quietly,' she says. I think of his voice echoing back out of the cave, the dark caves full of rock formations and things miners went down for. Sophe's made up great grandfather down there all day and missing the day because when he came up it would be dark. I know he wasn't her great grandfather but someone had to do it. Whoever it was they'd have had a miners lamp. I think of Ham turning into a rock that looks like a boy and becoming a story told by a guide in another million years time. Though we'd all be dead by then so it doesn't seem so bad.

We go back to see if he's in the Pub where we had the cokes. He isn't. Nina says she's going back to the car park in case he's looking for the car. Nina is looking worried. There's a family in front of us we rather push past, a woman with a push chair and a girl in a pink sunhat.

The pink sunhat turns round and says. 'Mattie,' like she was my best friend ever. Its Jasmine from the Zoo. I don't recognise her at first.

'Who's your friend Mat?' says John.

'Its Jasmine' I say remembering. 'We met at the Zoo.'

'You didn't recognise her,' says John in an accusing kind of way as though I thought all black people looked the same, which is stupid as they aren't even all the same colour. I didn't recognise Eva in St. Ives. I do feel bad about not recognising Jasmine though in case she thinks I've forgotten her already but she laughs and says, 'That's because I had my face painted like a tiger.'

'By the lion's cage' I say to show I did remember.

'Which could be confusing,' says Miles. John doesn't say anything.

John and Miles go up a lot of steps called Jacobs Ladder so they'll have a better view but they still can't see Ham.

I wonder why they don't tell the police, they would on television, but it seems they've done that before and it causes a lot of fuss and then he turns up and it wasn't as if there was a policeman around to tell.

'What if someone's taken him?' I ask as I don't think they're taking it seriously enough.

'They won't keep him for long.' says Miles.

'I'll go to the Pub with the girls again in case he's gone back there and you two go to the amusements again,' says Nina. A passing poodle brushes against my leg.

'The dog.' I say. 'What about the dog?'

'Yes, the talking dog. Good thinking.' says Miles. And we all go back down to where the dog was and its still there and Ham's still talking to it. Everyone's pleased and I'm pleased I thought of the dog because Miles says, 'We'll have to take Mattie with us everywhere, she's psychic.'

He takes a photo of Ham talking to the dog and its as though he wasn't lost as no one says anything to Ham and Ham certainly doesn't behave like he's been lost or found.

He comes over to us and walks through people as though they weren't there and I think of Failand saying he was like a ghost. Only he isn't because a man gets annoyed.

'Watch where you're going dumbo,' he says.

'Go and take an IQ test yourself.' says Failand surprisingly, sounding out of character. More like Sophe. Maybe she is like Sophe but somehow I don't think they'd get on.

'Leave it, we're all back together now,' says Nina who's looking relieved about finding Ham and I can see she was worried really.

'Lets have a family photo,' she says, in a while-we've-got-the-chance sort of way. I offer to take it with her camera. They get in a group with the rocks behind them. Hamish isn't looking till he's told to, then he stares like a Meercat.

'How many birds in the sky?' asks Miles.

'Seven,' says Hamish looking up as I take it. I press it to see and it's a good photo of everyone. Hamish doesn't look any different to the others. John does. Well it's a photograph, which only shows how people look not how they are.

'We'd better have one of Mattie to remember her.' Miles takes the camera and I think of being gone and never seeing any of them again and one day they'll see my photo and say, 'Who's that girl?' and Failand may say, she came down one summer it was the day we lost Ham. And Miles will say, 'We lost Ham every day.' Then he'll look at the photo and see the rocks and say, 'Its in Cheddar. Her name was Mattie,' and he'll remember kissing me by the pond. I am thinking this of me being the ghost of summer past and Miles says.

'Oh shit I've deleted it, I'll have to do another.'

But then man who called Ham a Dumbo comes out of a shop with a flagon of cider.

'I'm sorry,' he says, 'I didn't realise,'

'Realise what?' says John aggressively, 'You want to have some respect man,' and John doesn't sound like John more like Abe. But I don't think John and Abe would be friends anymore than Sophe and Failand.

'I'm sorry I…'the man is floundering and outnumbered. I wonder what has Ham done to convince him that he's a case for apologising, like he really is out of step but you can't say it if its true.

'Too late mate,' says Miles.

'Its totally understandable, Hamish doesn't look where he's going,' says Nina but to Miles and John not the man. I think how me and Sophe thought Clocker Wallace was a paedophile, when all he wanted was to know what the time was.

Ham is totally unconcerned about any of the fuss he's caused.

'No spatial awareness,' says Failand but as though it's a talent.

My phone rings but I don't notice it as it doesn't t ring very often.

'Your phone,' says Miles who must have more noise awareness than me.

'I expect its Sophe,' I say. I'm glad its rung so it looks like I've got friends of my own.

CHAPTER FIFTEEN

It isn't Sophe on the phone, its Grandad which is a surprise as he isn't the sort to phone and they know about me being out with Nina. Well Gran does. He sounds strange and I think what if something's happened to Ed. I feel a great fear, which isn't like being on a horse kind of fear but something bigger and sadder that isn't going to stop when you get off.

'Your Gran's been taken ill,' that's what he says, 'taken ill' and has had to go to hospital I'm there now. Could you wait next door till I get back.'

I feel relieved that it isn't Ed. I must have been more worried about Ed than I thought. Grandad is obviously worried about Gran to phone me. He doesn't like interfering.

'Whats wrong?'

'A stroke.' I feel my stomach go sort of funny as though I'm desperate to go to the toilet. Even though I'm not sure what a stroke is except its to do with heart attacks. The others are all looking at me as though I'd turned into Ham somehow. Like I might disappear and have to be looked for. I run to the Pub toilet and Nina follows me and asks if I'm alright. I just want her to go away. Going to the toilet is all I can think of.

When I come out they're all asking about Ed as though he'd died or something. I feel annoyed as though they'd written Ed off even though I had been thinking the same.

'No its my Gran she's had a stroke,' I say and it doesn't sound so bad when I say it. Perhaps its just something old people get all the time like high blood pressure and forgetting names and even cancer but seem to live with.

'We'd better get back,' Nina says, 'don't worry, lots of people get strokes, my Dad had about eight.' She doesn't say if he's still alive and I don't ask. I think of a cat having nine lives which might mean Gran's still got eight.

'Lets buy her a present.' Ham says, 'lets buy her some cheese.'

Nina says, 'Flowers,' and we find a proper flower shop and they've got a bucket full of blue flowers in the front. I ask for a bunch. When the girl gives them to me they don't look like the flowers in the bucket, like when you pick bluebells and they don't look like the bluebells in the wood. These aren't bluebells, I don't know what they're called.

'Let me get her some too,' says Nina and she buys two more bunches and puts them with mine and they look a lot better. I feel better too when I'm looking out of the car window and watching the sheep asleep in the fields like stones. Perhaps they're supposed to look like stones. That's their camouflage like crocodiles look like logs. I've never thought this before but I don't feel like bothering to say anything.

'Look at all those sheep, I wonder why they bothered to clone a sheep when they all look alike already,' says Miles.

'Like cloning zebras,' agrees John.

'They don't all look alike, some have got black faces,' I say and John laughs but in a nice way and Miles pats me on the back like I'd won something.

'What are they called?' I ask about the flowers to change the subject.

'Cornflowers,' says Failand, 'they make your eyes look really blue.' Everyone's being nice to me as if Gran had died but I think she'll be alright when I get back. It'll be like nothing's happened, like finding Ham. I almost hope it's a bit serious so I won't look as if I'm making a fuss about nothing. I look at my arm, my classic scratch is healing in little scabs. I scratch my scratch, my arm's going brown as if I'd been on a proper holiday.

My phone rings again and its Mum who's also heard about the stroke and says Dad's coming down on the train. I start worrying again as Dad wouldn't catch a train for nothing. It must be serious and Gran is his mother. I'm crying when I put the phone down.

'Don't cry Mattie,' says Ham patting me like he's talking to a cat and I think of the boy Danny by the river who's got a cat called Mattie and said my eyes looked blue. It makes me cry more, though it isn't sad.

'My Dad's coming down,' I say feeling like someone on television after a disaster, when people fly out to look for their dead relatives in the rubble. I know I'm being dramatic. I want to ring Sophe, but when I'm by myself. When Mum asked where I was and I said Cheddar though we'd left Cheddar she said, 'Did you tell Gran? Did she know you were going to Cheddar?' sounding worried. As though me going to Cheddar was enough to cause a stroke or did Mum think I'd gone off on my own? I told Mum she thought we were going to Weston but then we changed our minds. It was a mystery tour.

I remembered Gran not wanting to go to Cheddar and then I thought it had something to do with Christopher. And this time I knew I was right. I wanted to see Christopher so much I nearly said so as though he was a real person. Like he was still Gran's brother which he is. I mean if Ed. Not I can't think of Ed now.

When we got back it seems hard getting into the house as everyone wants me to go next door. I say I want to get a sweater as though I was cold. I do feel cold. Failand says she'll give me one of hers, she's got one that would suit me its too small for her. She's taller than me but not fatter. I don't think Failand will ever be fat. She says her Dad bought the sweater in Paris, broad stripes, blue and navy with a slash neck. I like the sound of it, mostly I like the sound of it being bought in Paris. I'm not sure what a slash neck is but I say I've got to get my own. It seems very important to see Christopher and I want to ring Sophe. At first I can't find the spare key that they keep under a big stone on a rockery with pink flowers. I'm panicking by now. There's this enormous bee as if it's guarding the key. Miles come to find it for me.

'The dragons den,' he says handing it to me and then, 'Don't worry she's going to be alright,' and gives me a little hug. Which I liked a lot but it still didn't mean he was right. I mean people do die, especially if they're old and have a stroke. Grans' not that old, 61 my other Gran is 67 and she's in Croatia with Saga holidays.

I run upstairs and almost call out to Christopher as soon as I get in the bedroom but he isn't there. I look in the wardrobe where the old books and box of dinky toys were and they're still there but more like a magic pebble the witch gives the child in a fairy story. When they wake up and everyone says it was a dream they've still got the pebble. I really want Christopher to be here, partly because I felt him not being here made it more likely Gran might be dead. I even go into Gran and Grandad's bedroom and there was a picture of Christopher in a leather frame. It was one I'd never seen before and it was one that looked just like him. Like how I knew him. It made it seem as though he'd turned back into a photograph and that was all he was. Marley was there brushing against my leg and mewing. I thought he was missing Christopher too, then I realised he was just hungry. Gran usually feeds him so I put out some cat food, that hard dry sort and feel responsible and as though I'd always lived here. I see my grey dress I was sick on ironed and hung up in the kitchen and I feel guilty, I haven't done much while I was here. I wil be veery helpful when Gran comes home if I'm not back at school. If I was at home and Gran had

had a stroke it wouldn't have seemed a big thing - well not so big. Just a phone call and mum saying your Gran's ill. I nearly forget to get a sweater then I grab a red jacket with a hood which Sophe said made me look like Little Red Riding Hood. I feel a bit like her anyway. I remember the cornflowers and pick them up. All I need is a wicker basket.

Nina gives me a cup of tea and a piece of chocolate cake, which I really enjoy. It makes me feel I couldn't be that worried till I remember the woman in Wells Cathedral café with the skull face eating a piece of chocolate cake. Being in Failand's house it doesn't feel Gran could be dead, not like it did in their empty house where even the ghost was gone. I wonder if I should say about Christopher, it seems a time when I could. Like at the end of the Christmas term when teachers talk like they're your best friends.

'Christopher isn't there,' I say and Nina looks at me like she's seen a ghost herself. Then Ham starts making a big fuss over a lost pen. I hand him a blue biro but he snaps it in half and says he wants a black one and sounds like a baby. They do tell him off this time. But I'm almost glad because all the others are being nice to me which makes me feel they know something I don't. When I first met Ham I said to Gran that they shouldn't treat him as if he's different. She said, 'But he is different.'

Their dog comes up to me all eager and pushes his nose in my face and I think how a dog is different to a cat. How they mind more.

I ring Sophe. She is there this time. She says, 'What is it? Is it Ed?' so I must sound as though something serious has happened.

'No its my Gran,' she's had a stroke, she just says, 'Oh,' as though that was alright then, as though having a stroke was something Nan's did. Not that Gran having a stroke makes Ed better though it feels like it should. Its like when you see a wildlife programme, you're feeling sorry for the rabbit all frozen with fear when the owl swoops down and you hope it'll get away. Sometimes it does. Then when you see the owl go back to its nest and the hungry owlets all waiting for their dinner you don't know who's side you're on.

I'm looking out of the window because this house has turned into a sort of prison. Then a taxi pulls up in the road and Dad gets out. I'm so glad, its like he's coming back from the war or something. He doesn't go to Gran's house but comes straight up the drive which has got pinky coloured bricks in a pattern. I run up to him like the girl in the Railway Children. He seems to bring my real life back with him, Yorkshire and Ed and Mum, and Spider and my bedroom. The others fade away like dreams in the morning. He kept the taxi for us to go to the hospital though Nina offers to drive.

'How's Ed?' I say in the taxi feeling a bit of a stranger again and trying to remember what's important.

'He's good and he's coming home and the Doctors are really pleased with him,' Dad sounds pleased too but distracted. He's thinking about Gran now, not Ed, like I'm thinking about being home not being here. It's early evening and a blackbird is singing in the hospital car park. I think how Gran will like that. The taxi driver says what a beautiful day it's been and had we been anywhere nice.

'Cheddar,' I say and it feels like everything's right with the world. I remember a poem, 'The snail's on the thorn all's right with the world,' which Mrs. James read out once and was all pleased with.

'You'de think she'd written it herself,' said Sophe. It was like once when Bill Oddie was getting all excited about a birds egg and Gran said 'he was crowing like he'd laid it himself.' Sophe wouldn't like to know she said what Nans say.

In the hospital I feel scared again it reminds me of when Ed was first diagnosed.

'She's going to be alright isn't she? and Dad looks preoccupied and says,

'Lets hope so.' instead of yes. Perhaps I'm making a fuss and of course people have strokes, like Nina's father.

'I shouldn't mention Cheddar,' says Dad.

'Why not?'

'She had a brother,' .

'I know.

'Has she spoken about him, that's good, she never did, he got lost in a cave when he was a boy. She was with him. She came back without him and they never found him. Christopher his name was. They couldn't even find the cave apparently. She never got over it.'

He says it simply like that. The whole story. I can't speak. I just stare at some pictures of hot air balloons on the wall wanting to be in one looking down on everything, not part of it. I want to go back to the house and find Christopher. Ask him where he is? Perhaps he'll tell me now, now all the rules are broken. If they could find the body he could rest in peace. He'd be like the caveman's skeleton only newer.

Grandad comes to join us looking worried and perhaps I shouldn't be worrying about a ghost when Gran is in intensive care.

'Its bad,' he says, 'very bad,' he's speaking to Dad who is his son, which isn't something I think about usually, that Grandad is Dad's Dad I mean.

'Perhaps they can do something, its amazing what they can do,' says Dad.

I think of Casualty and Holby City and all those TV programmes where they call in the team and get a heart beating again and the patient sits up.

Once Sophe said to Walter, the name on the war memorial, 'They could cure you now Walt, stitch you up, patch up your face with some skin off your bum.' It seemed funny at the time now it seems rude because Walter was a real person, a young man who didn't come home from the war. Like soldiers today who you see on the News who get killed in Iraq. I think of Christopher who didn't come home, who was there in a cave in the dark so he couldn't even see the rock formations, well unless he had a torch. He might have fallen over and broken his leg or something. He'd be thinking his sister Jenny was coming back with a cave rescue team to get him out. I thought of Gran feeling guilty all these years for leaving him, for not even being able to find the cave. I think of us looking for Ham but I realise it wasn't like that. Ham is different, he doesn't care, he wouldn't realise people were looking for him. He wouldn't feel lost. She might have expected Christopher to know what he was doing. He'd just passed the 11-plus which Gran failed and went to secondary modern school and left at fifteen. I don't think I could ever ask her about it even when she gets better, if she does get better. Maybe next year but next year has stopped feeling like something you can rely on.

'If only he'd had a mobile phone,' I say but Dad isn't listening.

'Can we see her?' he asks Grandad.

'She's gone for a scan,' says Grandad. I know about scans from Ed. I think a scan sounds like a good thing even it's only looking. A woman arrives and she is carrying a wicker basket with a big bunch of wild looking flowers. She's very fat and wearing a pale mac though it isn't raining. It makes her look like when they wrap up a whole building, a church tower or something for repairs. They'd stop her wearing it if it was a TV makeover, but it isn't and she doesn't seem to care and it suits her in an unflattering kind of way.

'How is she?' it turns out this is Linda who Gran went to the painting class with where she had the stroke. I'd forgotten about the painting class. Linda doesn't look a bit like Miss Marples.

My dad is talking to a nurse who has an Australian accent I think of my cousin Leanne who is a nurse in Australia. Its like they've swapped places. I seem to be noticing everything. Then I notice Christopher. He's not like when I see him in the bedroom, more like a painting by someone in a playgroup. Like a little child saying, 'This is my Mummy,' and it could be anybody but somehow it is their Mummy if they say so. I know its him or supposed to be him and I'm relieved.

'She's not dead,' I say like a fact not a question.

'Only the end of the world is the end of the world.' says Linda. Which sounds like it means something hopeful but maybe not for my Gran. It might not be the end of the world but it might be the end of Grans. I try to think of dying as something natural and ordinary like seeing lambs in the field who don't know they're going to be eaten, but it doesn't work. It's more like leaves falling off trees in Autumn, they're dead but the tree survives and grows new ones, which is better but it doesn't help much. I don't want a new leaf. In films or books when an old person dies someone has a baby. There is a woman with a baby in the waiting room. Its crying. I feel annoyed with it. It feels like an omen.

Dad and Grandad go in by themselves and come out looking pretty sick. I want to go in to take my flowers but they say I'd better wait till tomorrow. The Australian nurse takes them and promises to put them by her bed.

'It'll be the first thing she sees when she wakes up,' she says. I look across at the bed with the blue flowers as we leave, it looks like a picture on a get well card, except the bed is empty.

Christopher isn't in the house when we get back. My bedroom feels empty. I hear Dad ringing Mum and it sounds serious. But then I think it would sound serious. When Brian, down our road got cancer Mum and Dad talked as if he was dying and we stopped walking on his wall, but he's still there cutting his lawn and shouting at the kids who've gone back to walking on his wall. He doesn't look like he's going to die, well not for ages.

CHAPTER SIXTEEN

Next day Mum and Ed arrive in the car and its so good to see them. Just like old holidays when we came together to stay here in the summer and Ed didn't have leukaemia. We were like a separate family, sometimes we'd go off to Weston or Weymouth or even Lyme Regis without Gran or Grandad.

Feeling good doesn't last as Gran's had another stroke in the night. They go off to the hospital with Grandad and I stay with Ed. Then I tell him about Christopher. Not about him being a ghost, well not at first, I point out the photograph on the bookcase and say that was Gran's brother who died when he was about eleven and he says he knows.

'Oh of course I forgot you know everything,'

'He went down a cave on the Mendips and never came up,' he says casually as though it was something we talked about often, not like something I'd only just found out.

'Well I've seen him.'

'Where?'

'In my bedroom,'

'I expect its puberty,' and I wish he hadn't said that. As though seeing ghosts is like starting your periods.

'What d'you mean?' which is something I often say to Ed.

'I don't know?' which isn't something Ed says very often. Then he adds, 'like poltergeists.'

'Poltergeist?'

160

'Yes don't they only manifest themselves to girls?' Which makes me sound old fashioned, a Victorian girl who'd faint at the sight of blood and imagine boy ghosts because I was only interested in sex but had to pretend I preferred needlework.

'He's a real ghost he plays with dinky cars and makes model aeroplanes and …' I was going to say he can speak but I thought I'd said enough.

'Well I shouldn't go on about it you don't want to be diagnosed as schizophrenic.' I nearly say its better than having leukaemia. I liked Ed better when he wasn't here. I'm almost crying.

'OK introduce me,' he says. I think he's noticed I'm upset or is it because he always wants to prove things. Actually I've almost stopped believing in Christopher because Ed's making him sound like an illness. We go up to the bedroom and of course he isn't there.

'That's the trouble with ghosts you can never find one when you want one,' he says as I apologise. I show him the old books and the box with the dinky toys.

'No wonder you're imagining things, sleeping in a museum.' The toys do look like the one's in the toy museum in Cheddar. He says Gran shouldn't have hoarded them. But I feel I have to stick up for her.

'Don't say that. What if she dies?'

'Well she is old,'

'She's not old,' I say crossly, 'Mrs Wooley is old, anyway people live longer today and women live longer than men you should see the gravestones. She had her hair doen yesterday,' I say remembering and want start to cry.'

'Well she's had a life, not like Leo. He was thirteen,' I remember his friend in hospital who died and Ed's leukaemia that might come back even if he is in remission. I suppose having a stroke when you're sixty one doesn't sound so bad.

'Christopher was young,' I say.

'Forget Christopher,' he says as though he doesn't matter because he's been dead for so long. Like the names on the cenotaph to me and Sophe. I think being in hospital has changed Ed and maybe things will never be the same again even if Gran gets better. I suppose Mum would just say. 'You're both growing up.' Growing up feels like part of you is dying.

Ed is fiddling with a toy plane.

'Balsa wood,' he says and floats it across the room and I wish Christopher could see it. As though he hadn't been dead all this time, down a cave like the old skeleton who's just a bit of history in a glass case. But right now it feels like he's just died, died again I mean. I say this to Ed to try to make him see the ghost as an idea even if he wasn't there.

'Like stopping believing in God,' he says, as though he's stopped. Perhaps its because of Leo dying in hospital. If you stop believing in something it must mean you thought it was never there in the first place which isn't the same as something disappearing.

'It must have been dreadful.' I say not knowing if I mean Leo dying or Ed being in hospital and having to have life saving treatment. I want to say did you think you might die. But I don't.

'It was like being in a shoot out.' he says, 'you feel threatened and you might really be shot if you make a wrong move but part of you thinks its not true like the guns a replica or its just a game. And then,' - he stops.

'And then?' I say thinking its alright now.

'And then your mate gets shot and he's really dead even if you get away, this time,' he says bitterly and I realise why he's not so worried about Gran as I am.

Mum and Dad and Grandad come back and say Gran has died. We all sit around in silence. I don't cry. I feel sick. I am sick. I think of the barbecue when I was sick and Gran seemed a bit drunk herself and I still don't cry. I go up to my bedroom just in case Christopher is there. I don't want to have to tell him. He isn't, and I didn't think he would be because he belonged to Gran. I realise that now even though she didn't know he was there. Not like I did. Perhaps he was in her mind and she was thinking about him and her thoughts came through to me somehow, telepathy or even a sixth sense. I want to say Goodbye but I know its too late. For Christopher I mean, well it was always too late for Christopher.

Downstairs they're talking about Gran. Grandad's ringing his sister in Canada, the one on the photo. Mum's ringing her mother, my other Gran. I don't ring Sophe. I have an awful feeling she might say, its what Nans do, then I'd never be able to speak to her again and I will want to but not now. Now doesn't seem real, nothing does. Mum says lets go out and get something to eat. We go to an Indian restaurant that doesn't seem real either. Its called the Taj Mahal but it doesn't look like the picture. Grandad says he can remember when it was a Pub. I want to say how it was usually Gran who remembered how things used to be, like Rosie at the Zoo but I don't because I can't say her name now, like before I couldn't mention Christopher.

'This was the lounge bar,' he says, 'there was a picture of the cricket team on the wall. I was in it.' There's a picture of elephants on the wall now with things elephant's wear in India and elephant jewellery on.

'The elephant in the lounge bar,' says Ed.

'They're all dressed up,' I say.

'Yes they're dressed up as Indians,' says Ed. He thinks I mean the waiters who are wearing Indian clothes, though I meant the elephants.

'Jen always wanted to come here but I don't really like curry,' says Grandad. We've got a table and the Indian waiters are being friendly and its almost like a celebration not Gran being dead.

'She liked a change,' he says sadly as though he'd failed to make changes. Ed smiles and I have a horrible feeling he's going to say that she was changed now. And I thought how she wasn't just not here, missing a curry. And being pleased about Ed being out of hospital but everything. Not just like Ham not going to mainstream school or even a refugee and turned out of your country. More like when people can't pay the mortgage and have their house repossessed, Gran's had her life repossessed.

Grandad finishes his curry and says he liked it and I know he's thinking how he should have come here with Gran. Mum says you always feel like that when someone dies. When her Dad died one Christmas they hadn't even gone round with his present the night before like they meant to because they were going to a party. They hadn't even wrapped it.

'What was it?' asks Ed.

'Cancer,' says Mum, you remember don't you.

'The present,' he says and it sounds like a bad joke

'Oh only a shirt, and I know he'd never have got to wear it. That wasn't the point,' says Mum wearily. I was glad Ed didn't ask if they'd taken it back.

We stay on and go to the funeral. All her friends are there, Wendy and Linda and the woman who sang at the jazz Pub and Josh's Grandfather from Nemphet Thrubwell and old Charlie, Ham's great grandfather who remembered Gran's mother, Elsie my great grandmother. Nina and Toby are there but not Hamish. I expect he's with Maria. Failand and Miles aren't, they're in Paris with their biological father and his French partner and French baby. I think of them being on the river Seine in a boat like we went on when we went to Paris with the school. I wonder if they were thinking of us and Jenny, their next door neighbour being dead or just saying, 'You can see the Eiffel Tower from here.'

People say nice things about Gran and things they'd done with her and places they'd been and it felt Gran had a full life and didn't miss much except old age. Then the coffin disappears and I think of her going into the cave with Christopher. Perhaps she was scared of the dark and not thinking of him, well not till after she's got out herself. Then when he's never found again she has to think of him all the time.

When we go outside there's a hot air balloon going over. It disappears quite quickly like hot air balloons do. And when we get back to the house someone rings Grandad to say his car has been found. Its been found abandoned in Nenphett Thrubwell. It feels like life is moving on without Gran in it.

Grandad's sister Pat is over from Canada. Somehow it's more like she's on holiday as she's been in Canada for ages and keeps going on about how everything's 'changed in the UK.' I think of the book called 'Jandy Mac Comes Back.'

'Well except in this house,' she says and talks about when Gran and Grandad got married and she was a bridesmaid and so was Gran's sister Jackie. They wore orange dresses which the woman who made them called apricot and its happy talk. Then Marley walks in and she says something disturbing. Well disturbing to me.

'It's the same cat. I remember the cat, we tried to tie a yellow ribbon round its neck but it kept tearing it off, it can't be the same one, it must have given up the ghost by now.' I think of the ribbon in her hair when she was sat on the doorstep in the photograph. I now think of it as a yellow ribbon, the cats ribbon even. It couldn't have been as she was only about seven in the picture. But that isn't what I find disturbing. It's as if the cat I saw with Christopher wasn't Marley but another cat. The cat who wouldn't wear his bow at the wedding. A ghost cat after all?

'This is Marley the fourth,' says Grandad and it doesn't seem to matter. Like they've all joined up like the tigers who ran round a tree till they melted into butter in an old children's book I found in the wardrobe. Maybe it could be an Oak tree and they could all turn into a yellow ribbon like in that song.

I can't believe Gran's going to be just a name on a stone in the churchyard like the ones she used to know. Nor can I believe she'll meet Jackie and Christopher. Just not here, like Miles and Failand. And I'll probably never see them again either.

When we get back home it seems even more like a dream. We stayed at the house till after the funeral. Dad asked Grandad to come back and stay with us but he said he'd sooner stay at his house where his friends are and his memories. Anyway Pat's still there. When we went she was clearing out things. I expect she'll throw the old toys away or give them to a charity shop. Will other children play with them? I don't think it matters anymore. I don't think they'll be any ghosts in that house now. I've got a picture Gran painted of Marley. Or is it the cat before? I know its not the cat who wouldn't wear his ribbon because Gran wouldn't have been painting then.

I'm glad I'm back at home though, because it doesn't seem so bad about Gran dying as it would if I was still there and Gran wasn't there and Christopher never appeared again. I don't mean she's taken him with her or they're together again. Just both gone like in a disaster when whole families get wiped out. Grandad asked if we wanted any photographs. Dad said we had plenty but I looked through the album and took the one of Gran when she was girl with her sister Jackie and her mother Elsie who old Charlie can still remember. Its got the pram in the background with Christopher in it and his whole life in front of him even if he doesn't quite get to my age.

Though we're all sad about Gran we're all glad about Ed. I realise how worried Mum and Dad have been. Its almost like Gran's saved him. Not like if she'd gone back down in the cave and found her brother. Nor because she's dead herself as though the world was a bus with only so many empty seats so Gran's had to give up her seat for other people to get on. Its no good, it doesn't help. I think how much liked to find a seat.

I know lots of people die together in famines and plagues and wars which might upset the balance of nature. I don't think it does because there's so many of us. Its more like it puts it right if we die because the world isn't big enough and there's not enough trees or icebergs.

Once in school Mr. Allan was trying to explain biodiversity.

'If we had less doctors trying to cure people and feed the hungry it would sort itself out,' said Nathan. It did seem to make sense but Mr. Allan said how we were a social species despite everything and felt obliged to pick up the baby on our doorstep most of the time. I thought of leaving a baby on a doorstep like they say you shouldn't interfere with baby birds if they fall out of the nest. I think even Nathan would pick it up. If Ed hadn't gone to hospital, he might be dead by now. I think of Christopher still down his cave, well his bones. I suppose its what people call the bigger picture and its too big for me to see it all. Back in Mrs. James's class she reads out my story, she calls it a story as if it wasn't true.

The class went quiet at the end. Sophe shrugs. I suppose she thinks I made it up like being at the Taj Mahal. I think Mrs. James does too as she says I have a vivid imagination. She approves of vivid imaginations, making things up, which is not to be confused with telling lies.

'I wonder what really happened to the ghost?' Abe comes up to me afterwards and he sounds as if he really did wonder. Believed I'd seen him anyway.

'Respect, at last,' said Sophe, who didn't.

'It just disappeared,' I said lamely.

'Its what ghosts do,' said Nat who likes to sound like an expert on everything even my Grans brother's ghost. I wish I'd kept him a secret but its too late now. People tell tales. I wrote this one for my Gran and my Gran's brother's ghost.

THE END

ELAINE EVELEIGH

14 Providence Lane,

Long Ashton,

Bristol. BS41 9DQ.

Tel. 01275 393859.

elaineceveleigh@gmail.com

Printed in Great Britain
by Amazon.co.uk, Ltd.,
Marston Gate.